rhyme

&

reason

anita haigh

 SCRIPTURE UNION

Dedicated to the memory of Brenda D Anderson

Scripture Union, 207–209 Queensway, Bletchley, MK2 2EB, England.

© Anita Haigh 1996

First published 1996

ISBN 1 85999 036 3

British Library Cataloguing-in-Publication Data
A catalogue record for this book is available from the British Library.

Cover design by Mark Carpenter Design Consultants.
Cover illustration and illustrations by Helen Anderson.

Printed and bound in Great Britain by Cox & Wyman Ltd, Reading.

CONTENTS

Introduction	4
Key Letters	6
Title Index	7
Theme Index	8
Bible Index	9
General Pieces	11
Christmas Pieces	70
Easter Pieces	91

ACKNOWLEDGEMENTS

I would like to thank everyone who contributed to this book with material, ideas, helpful criticism, encouragement and practical guidance. Without their help, it couldn't have been written. All the material is original and used with the authors' permission.

For their ideas and material: Helen Anderson, Heidi Baron, Connie Cooke, Justin Fielder, Nick Haigh, Karen Hall, Samantha Johnson, Hannah Jowett, Fiona Langlands, Wayne Raper, Carolyn Rowland-Jones, Gavin Silver and Andrew Smith.

For their helpful comments: the staff members of Scripture Union, and students from the following schools in Cleveland – Acklam Grange, Bishopsgarth, Blakeston, Norton, Our Lady and St Bede, and Rosecroft.

Many thanks to Helen Anderson for the original artwork, and to Angela Pelley for typing the manuscript.

Finally, special thanks to my husband, Nick, for his encouragement and support.

INTRODUCTION

The background

This collection of sketches, raps, poems and monologues is based on the life and teaching of Jesus as they are depicted in the Gospels. The material was largely written for use in schools, during my time as a schools worker with Scripture Union and as a teacher taking RE lessons and assemblies.

The need to generate my own material grew out of the views about the Bible that I came across in schools. Phrases like 'Jesus said...' or 'The Bible says...', when they are used in an assembly hall or classroom, tend to have a 'switch off' effect as far as the audiences are concerned! For many young people, the Bible appears dull, boring, irrelevant or difficult to understand. So I have set out to explore the issues and questions raised by the gospel story in a culturally relevant way.

Some of the items simply re-tell a parable in a modern setting. Others reflect on specific aspects of Jesus' sermons or his encounters with different people. It is hoped that the material will be thought-provoking and encourage people to reason out Jesus' message for themselves. Hence, the book's title – **Rap, Rhyme & Reason**.

The pieces have been tried and tested in numerous schools by teachers and schools workers. Many have also been used successfully in family services, youth meetings and holiday clubs.

The aim

The aim of this book is two-fold:

1 To encourage young people to reflect on key issues that affect all human beings, such as justice, forgiveness, anger, fear and faith.

In the Gospels Jesus addresses issues like these, and his teaching is practical, incisive and sometimes uncomfortable! He challenges complacency, false religion and injustice. I have tried to write or select pieces which reflect his passion and directness of speech. My experience has shown that this approach is understood and welcomed by those listening.

2 To provide teachers, schools workers and youth workers with a resource that is credible, flexible and easy to use.

Most items need little in the way of rehearsal or props. They are easy to deliver and lend themselves to pupil involvement.

Using this book

Each piece is laid out in a simple format with a **key letter** (see page 6) indicating its suitability for particular age groups. The main target age is 11–14s, although several pieces can be used with older teens and adult audiences. There are guidelines as to the number of people and any props that are needed, as well as easy-to-follow performance directions. In most cases, learning the material by heart is not necessary – it can be performed just as effectively with script in hand!

The raps do need a little more preparation and rehearsal. They are written with four beats to a bar. To show how the verses fit the rhythm, the first beat of a bar is highlighted by a word in bold text. A drum machine or synthesizer would be helpful for keeping the beat, but is not essential.

The **key theme(s)** is given at the beginning of each piece, along with the **Bible passage(s)** to which it relates. These enable the key point(s) to be drawn out in a manner appropriate to the performance setting. Alternatively, the piece can be used simply as a catalyst for thought and reflection.

There are three indexes under which the material is listed:

- The **Title Index** is divided into three main sections: General Pieces, Christmas Pieces and Easter Pieces. The titles are listed alphabetically.

- The **Theme Index** is based on the most common topics in Jesus' teaching and key events in his life. This is particularly useful if you are following a thematic scheme in your own teaching programme.

- The **Bible Index** lists the Gospel passages on which each piece is based. This is helpful if you are studying a particular Gospel, or if you wish to follow up a theme in greater depth.

Finally, some names and places mentioned in the material may need to be adapted to suit your own geographical location or the current youth scene! Please feel free to change as appropriate. In most cases, I have indicated where such an alteration might be necessary. Above all, I hope that you and the young people you work with will enjoy using this material.

KEY LETTERS

L Most suitable for Lower Secondary age range (11–13s)

U Most suitable for Upper Secondary age range (14+) and adults

A Suitable for all ages (11+) including adult audiences

TITLE INDEX

General Pieces

1	A Calming Influence	11
2	Actions Speak Louder Than Words	16
3	'Arfer' (The Lord's Prayer)	18
4	Ballad of the Great Banquet	20
5	Ballad of the Rich Fool	22
6	Bully for You!	24
7	Elder Son Rap	25
8	Fast Food	27
9	Follow Me	29
10	Follow the Maker's Instructions	30
11	Forgiving or Forgetting?	33
12	Heart, Soul & Mind	34
13	Hypocrisy is…	36
14	I've Got My Rights	37
15	Love in the Twenty-first Century	38
16	Love of Money, The	40
17	Man Who Walks on Water, The	42
18	March for Justice	44
19	Mercy Triumphs over Judgement	45
20	Mobile Chippy Burger Bar Association, The	47
21	Modern Parable of the Good Samaritan	49
22	Mouth Almighty	52
23	Outcast	54
24	Parable of Norbutt and Cedric, The	55
25	Postman Pat Delivers Good News	58
26	Rich Young Ruler	61
27	Story of Dertie Balloon, The	62
28	Story of Julian, The	64
29	That's Not Fair!	66
30	Time Rap	67
31	Zack Rap	69

Christmas Pieces

32 Christmas Rapping   70
33 Low-budget Nativity Play   72
34 Mary's Visitor   76
35 Nativity, The   79
36 Rock the Manger   89

Easter Pieces

37 Beginning, The   91
38 Betrayal – Judas   93
39 Denial – Peter   94
40 Kisses   96

THEME INDEX

Numbers in bold refer to item number.

Accountability **14, 28**
Anxiety **30**
Betrayal **38, 39, 40**
Bullying **6, 22, 29**
Christmas **32, 33, 34, 35, 36**
Compassion **21**
Easter **37, 38, 39, 40**
Fairness **7, 18, 23, 29**
Faith **1, 8, 17, 39**
Fear **1**
Forgiveness **11**
Greed **5, 16**
Hypocrisy **13**
Jesus' authority **1, 17, 20**
Judgementalism **19**
Justice **18, 23**
Love, the greatest commandment **12, 15**

Miracles **1, 8, 17, 20**
Obedience **2, 34**
Parables **2, 4, 5, 7, 10, 14, 21, 23, 24, 25, 26, 27, 28**
Peer pressure **9**
Prayer **3**
Priorities **2, 4**
Rejection **23**
Respect for others **14, 22, 23, 29**
Response to God **4, 31, 34**
Responsibility **14, 28, 29**
Role models **9**
Selfishness **2, 5, 14, 16, 28**
Time **30**
True security **5, 26, 27, 31**
Wealth **5, 16, 26, 27, 31**

BIBLE INDEX

Numbers in bold refer to item number.

Matthew

chs 1 & 2 **33 35**	1:18–25 **32**
5:21–22 **22**	5:43–48 **6**
6:1–4 **13**	6:9–13 **3**
6:19–24 **16**	6:25–34 **30**
7:24–29 **10 24**	8:23–27 **1**
12:33–37 **22**	13:1–9 **25**
14:14–21 **8 20**	14:22–23 **17**
18:21–35 **11**	21:28–32 **2**
22.35–40 **12 15**	25:31–46 **23 28**
26:14–16,20–25,47–50 **37 38**	26:69–75 **39**

Mark

4:35–41 **1**	14:10–11,17–21,43–46 **38**
12:28–31 **15**	14:66–72 **39**
14:43–49 **40**	

Luke

1:26–38 **32 34**	ch 2 **33 35**
2:1–20 **32**	4:16–19 **18 29**
5:27–32 **9**	6:27–28, 32–36 **6**
6:46–49 **10**	7:36–50 **19**
8:22–25 **1**	10:25–28 **15**
10:25–37 **21**	11:2–4 **3**
12:16–21 **5 27**	14:16–24 **4**
15:25–32 **7**	18:18–24 **26**
19:1–10 **31**	19:11–27 **14**
22:1–6,21–22,47–49 **38**	22:54–62 **39**

John
14:6 **33**

1 Corinthians
ch 13 **15**

A CALMING INFLUENCE
a sketch

> **Key: A**
> **Themes:** Faith, Fear, Jesus' authority, Miracles
> **Based on:** Matthew 8:23–27; Mark 4:35–41; Luke 8:22–25
> (Jesus calms a storm)

Props
A table (laid with cloth, cutlery, flowers) & 4 chairs
A jug of water and 2 glasses
Other tables similarly laid out (if extras are used)
Menus
An apron for Esther to wear
A 'cabbage' sandwich

Characters
Esther, the waitress
David & Dorcas, a couple in the cafe
Peter, a disciple
Andrew, a disciple
If there are extras, these can be other customers

Scene
Esther's Eating House. David and Dorcas sit at the main table, studying the menus. There are two glasses and a jug of water on the table in front of them. Esther hovers around, doing waitressy type things.

David:	(*Calling*) Esther, Esther!
	(*Esther comes over to table.*)
Esther:	Good evening, David. What can I get you?
David:	Well, I think I would like a nice piece of fish lightly grilled, thank you.
Esther:	Oooh, that could be tricky. With that violent storm today not many fish got caught. But I can do you a nice cabbage sandwich.

Dorcas: Do you have any sprouts, Esther?

Esther: I think so, Dorcas, but I'll have to check.

Dorcas: If you have got some, I'll have a Brussels-sprout burger, please.

David: I'll have two of your cabbage sandwiches with plenty of mustard.

Esther: OK, I'll be right back.

(She exits to the kitchen. David pours both himself and Dorcas a glass of water. They are about to start drinking when there are sounds of revelry and singing from outside the cafe which gradually get louder.)

Dorcas: What IS that noise?

David: It's those stupid fishermen. It sounds like they've been partying all day because they couldn't go out in the storm. Let's hope they don't come in here.

(As he says this the door bursts open. Peter and Andrew enter, laughing and singing very loudly and tunelessly with appropriate actions.)

Peter & *(Singing)* Row row row your boat
Andrew: Gently on the sea...
Merrily merrily merrily merrily
Home in time for tea!

Andrew: Hey, David! Good to see you! How you doing?

David: Well, I was doing very well until you two loud mouths burst in here.

Peter: Oh lighten up, Dave. We're only having a bit of fun.

Dorcas: By the sounds of it that's all you've been doing today.

David: Just because a little bit of bad weather stopped you going fishing, you think you can sit around fooling about.

Peter: Now whatever gave you that idea?

Dorcas: Esther told us that no one had been fishing today because of that storm.

Andrew: Oh she did, did she? Well, I think we're going to have to put the record straight here, aren't we, Peter?

Peter: We most certainly are. (*Calling*) Esther, Esther!
(*Esther enters carrying a cabbage sandwich.*)

Esther: Here you are, David, your cabbage sandwich.

Peter & Cabbage sandwich! Eeergh!
Andrew: (*They both pretend to be sick.*)

Esther: Oh stop mucking about, you two! What do you want?

Andrew: We wondered if you wanted to buy some fish to sell to your lovely customers?

Esther: I'd love to but where can I get any? That storm meant that no one went fishing today.

Peter: That's where you're wrong. Most fishermen stayed at home, but we were out there battling against the elements.

Dorcas: How can you have been? That storm was so strong you would surely be drowned by now!

Peter: Normally, yes. But we had the most extraordinary trip.

Andrew: Yeah, we'll tell you about it.
(*The disciples push Esther into a chair and turn Esther, Dorcas and David round so they are all facing the audience. Throughout this next part Esther, Dorcas and David keep protesting and trying to escape. Andrew and Peter keep acting out the story with great pace and energy so that they are unable to. It should be loud and fast but remain clear.*)

Peter: We started rowing out to sea, when it was fairly calm.
(*They rock Esther, Dorcas and David from side to side as if in a boat.*)

Andrew: In the front of the boat was Jesus.
(*Peter sits in front of them all.*)

Andrew: But he was worn out and he fell asleep.
(*Peter falls over and starts snoring for a few seconds. He then leaps up.*)

Peter: But then the wind started blowing stronger.
(*Andrew makes the noise of the wind and ruffles Dorcas' hair.*)

13

Peter: It blew stronger and stronger.

(*Andrew's wind noises get louder, and the two disciples start to push the three harder amidst increasing protests.*)

Andrew: Then it started to rain!

(*Peter picks up one of the glasses from the table and flicks water at the three captives. They scream as he does this.*)

Andrew: (*Shouting*) The rain got harder and harder and the wind blew stronger.

(*More screams as Peter flicks more and more water. He then picks up the jug of water and starts swinging it around as if he is going to throw it all over them.*)

Andrew: The waves got higher and higher, and we all thought we were going to drown. One really big wave started coming towards us.

(*Peter backs off a bit and gets ready to take a run up to throw all the water over Esther, Dorcas and David. They scream louder. Peter starts to runs towards them during Andrew's next speech. They scream even louder, so that Andrew is yelling over the noise. It wants to reach a crescendo as Andrew says, 'Jesus shouted…' At this point Peter should be about to throw the water.*)

Andrew: We all thought we were going to drown as the wave came nearer. Then someone thought to wake up Jesus, and just as the wave got to us Jesus shouted 'Be still…'

(*There is a pause. Peter doesn't throw the water. Esther, Dorcas and David stop screaming.*)

Andrew: (*Lowers his voice to almost a whisper.*) Then the wind and the waves just stopped. The storm just ended when he said that.

Peter: We carefully rowed back to shore. And we brought back the fish we had caught. Would you like some?

(*Dorcas, David and Esther are all looking very ill.*)

Dorcas: Actually, I don't feel very well. I think I might just go home.

David: It's funny, but I'm also feeling queasy. I'll just be running along.
(*They both exit, staggering and holding on to each other.*)

Peter: Funny couple. He didn't even eat his cabbage sandwich.

Esther: Did that really happen?

Andrew: Yeah, amazing isn't it?

Esther: I mean, he just said that, then the storm stopped.

Peter: You've got it.

Esther: But what sort of man is this? (*They freeze. The end.*)

2   ACTIONS SPEAK LOUDER THAN WORDS
a rap

Key: L
Theme: Parables, Priorities, Obedience
Based on: Matthew 21:28–32 (The parable of the two sons)

Words in **bold** indicate first beat in the bar. Words in CAPITALS said by chorus of voices.

Gather round you all and **listen** up SMART.
Gonna **tell** you all a story 'bout a **guy** named BART.
Now **he** was a farmer who **owned** a lot of LAND,
Making **wine** for a living with two **sons** to lend a HAND.

Now **Nigel** was the eldest, and in**clined** to be a FOOL,
With the **manners** of a monkey and the **temper** of a MULE.
His **dad** had asked him nicely, 'Please **go** and prune the VINES.
Then we'll **have** some juicy grapes to **make** some tasty
    WINES.'

But **Nigel** threw a wobbler – hard **work** was not his SCENE.
He'd **rather** watch the soccer on the **television** SCREEN.
But **as** he stormed out of the room, he **knew** that he'd done
    WRONG,
So he **went** and got a pruning knife and **put** his wellies ON.

Now **Kevin** was the younger son, a **smart** and clever LAD.
He **knew** exactly what to say to **get** around his DAD.
His **dad** had asked him nicely, 'Please **go** and prune the VINES.
Then we'll **have** some juicy grapes to **make** some tasty
    WINES.'

Well, **Kevin** smiled so sweetly, it **made** you want to SPEW!
'Of **course** I'll go,' he lied. ''Cos I'd do **anything** for YOU!'
But he **crept** up to his bedroom and he **switched** the TV ON.
He **thought,** 'Dad won't check up on me, 'cos **I'm** his
    fav'rite SON!'

The **question** is – who pleased his Dad and **did** just what
he OUGHT?
Bad-**tempered** Nige who changed his mind, or **Kev** – all
mouth and TALK?
Now **Jesus** told this story 'cos he **wants** us to OBEY.
It's **what** you DO that really counts, and **not** just what you
SAY.

© Anita Haigh 1992

3 'ARFER' (THE LORD'S PRAYER)
a short sketch

Key: A
Theme: Prayer
Based on: Matthew 6:9–13; Luke 11:2–4

Props

2 white shirts
2 school ties
2 school bags
Notepad and pencil

Characters

2 school pupils

Enter 2 pupils wearing shirts and school ties, bags slung over shoulders. Pupil 2 carries notepad and pencil, and jots down bits of the prayer when (s)he remembers them.

Pupil 1: So?

Pupil 2: So what?

Pupil 1: So what did he want to see you about then?

Pupil 2: Well, you know that Open Day's next week…

Pupil 1: What? The one the Mayor's coming to and that?

Pupil 2: Yeah! Well, I've got to do that bit in assembly.

Pupil 1: What bit?

Pupil 2: You know, that bit we do at the end about Arfer.

Pupil 1: Arfer?

Pupil 2: I think I know it off by heart. Listen! It goes 'Ar-fer … whose aunt's in heaven…'(*Scribbles in notepad.*)

Pupil 1: Is she? Which aunt's that then?

Pupil 2: 'Hello! Bee is thy name…'

Pupil 1: (*Interrupts*) Oh, so your Aunt Bee's dead then?

Pupil 2: (*Annoyed by interruptions*) 'Vikings they come …' (*Jots in notepad.*)

Pupil 1: Eh?

Pupil 2: 'Thy Will, he was done in on earth … and now is in heaven…'

Pupil 1: What? Arfer's Uncle Will was ·done in by the Vikings? Cor, he must've been older than I thought!

Pupil 2: Shhh, I'm trying to think! '…Give us this day our daily bread…'

Pupil 1: My mum says wholemeal's best 'cos it's got lots of fibre and it keeps you nice and regular…

Pupil 2: 'And give us our bus passes…' (*Jots in notepad*) '… as we forgive the buses that passed us…'

Pupil 1: I ain't forgiving 'em! Two hours I stood in the rain last week!

Pupil 2: 'Leave us not in the bus station…'

Pupil 1: Too right! It ain't half smelly in there!

Pupil 2: 'But deliver us from weevils…'

Pupil 1: Oh yeah! You get them on ships. We did about them in history, remember?

Pupil 2: (*Still jotting notes*) '…For why is the King's mum in power with the Tories?'

Pupil 1: What ARE you on about? We haven't got a King, we've got a Queen! Anyway, she's not in charge – it's that John Major bloke. (*Or the current Prime Minister.*)

Pupil 2: 'Said Hevver to Arfer, "Now then!"…' (*Makes final notes with a flourish!*)

Pupil 1: Who's Hevver? And why do we always have to say this at the end of assembly anyway?

Pupil 2: I dunno, but it's a good job I remembered it properly, else I'd look a right wally in front of the Mayor, wouldn't I?!

Pupil 1: (*Teasing*) You always look a right wally. Anyway, how's it go again?

(*Both exit reciting from notepad, 'Ar-fer, who's aunt's in heaven. Hallo! Bee is thy name…'*)

© Justin Fielder, Anita Haigh, Samantha Johnson, Carolyn Rowland-Jones 1992
Appeared in *OPEN LINES*, Vol 2 No. 2

4   **BALLAD OF THE GREAT BANQUET**
a poem with attitude!

Key: A
Themes: Parables, Priorities, Response to God
Based on: Matthew 22:1–14; Luke 14:15–24 (The parable of the great banquet)

Poem recited in dead-pan, assertive manner (á la Hale & Pace, 'The Management') to give impact.
    Each verse said by one person. Words in CAPITALS said by chorus of voices.

Jesus told a story 'bout a man who threw a PARTY.
He sent some invitations out 'cos he was quite a SMARTIE.
But they all made their excuses,
'Hey man, I've bought a car
And I've got to try it out
'COS IT'S A TURBO-POWERED FERRA—RI!'

Another said, 'I'm sorry, pal – don't mean to cause OFFENCE
But I've just negotiated on a high-class RESIDENCE.
It's a penthouse suite in… (*any desirable residential area*)
And it's got some lovely views
And I've got to check it out
'COS I'VE JUST FITTED A JACUZ—ZI!'

Still another said, 'Can't make it - I've got meself a WIFE
And it takes a lot of sorting, settling into married LIFE.
We need time to be together,
Just the two of us alone.
We're not ready yet for parties,
SO PLEASE DON'T EVEN PHONE—ME!'

Well, the man who sent the invites out was miffed at such
    EXCUSES.
Each one had got an invite and each one they had
    REFUSED HIS
Offer of a party.
So he asked in all the poor,
The lame, the blind, the crippled.
NOW TO FINISH OFF ME STOR—Y!

To those who had refused he said, 'Then you'll not taste my
    WINE.
I wanted you to have the best, to share all that is MINE.
But you went into your houses
And bolted up the door,
But your party will be over
WHEN I COME BACK IN GLOR—Y!

'Yes, your party will be over,
YOUR PARTY WILL BE OVER,
YOUR PARTY WILL BE OVER
When I come back once more!'

© Anita Haigh 1992

5 BALLAD OF THE RICH FOOL

Key: A
Themes: Greed, Parables, Selfishness, True security, Wealth
Based on: Luke 12:16–21 (The parable of the rich fool)

Recite in dead-pan, assertive manner (á la Hale & Pace, 'The Management') .

Each verse said by one person. Words in CAPITALS said by chorus of voices.

Listen to this story Jesus told about a FOOL
Who, 'cos he had a lot of dosh, thought he was dead COOL.
He owned a hundred acres of large and fertile fields
And with his P-reg tractor (*or current reg*) PLANTING
    CROPS WAS NO BIG DEAL.

But he had a dilemma – his barns were far too SMALL
And his harvest was a bumper one – where would he keep
    it ALL?
I know what I will do,' he said, 'I'll tear my old ones down
And build the biggest-ever barn, THE ENVY OF THE
    TOWN!'

'All the windows I put in will be UPVC
And I'll fit an anti-theft device for more SECURITY.
I'll put my name in neon lights to show who owns the lot
And there I'll stash away my crops AND EVERYTHING
    I'VE GOT!'

And feeling very satisfied he poured a glass to TOAST
Himself for all that he had done – 'I've got a right to BOAST!
For all my great achievements, I raise this glass of sherry
And now I'll take life easy – I'LL EAT, DRINK AND BE
    MERRY!'

But then he heard the voice of God – 'You fool, do you not
    KNOW
This night you'll die and then, my friend, where will your
    riches GO?
And all these things that you hold dear, in which you've
    placed your trust
Will then be taken from you AND LEFT TO ROT AND
    RUST!'

So the moral of this story is plain for all to SEE,
That worldly riches cannot give a lasting GUARANTEE.
A man's true life is not made up of things that he might
    own,
But everlasting treasure IS FOUND WITH GOD ALONE.

© Anita Haigh 1991

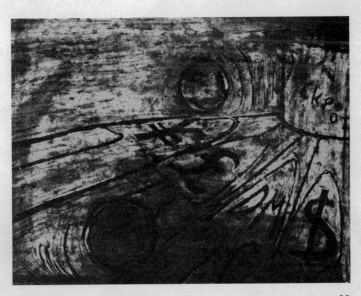

6   BULLY FOR YOU!
a rap

Key: L
Theme: Bullying
Based on: Matthew 5:43–48; Luke 6:27–28,32–36 (Love your enemies)

Each verse said by one person. Chorus said by alternating voices. Words in **bold** indicate first beat in the bar.

Chorus

Voice 1:   **Bully** boy, bully girl, **where** have you been?
Voice 2:   I've **been** in the playground **causing** a scene.
Voice 1:   **Bully** boy, bully girl, **what** did you there?
Voice 2:   I **beat** up a new boy and **pulled** out his hair.
Voice 1:   **Bully** boy, bully girl, **what** happened then?
Voice 2:   I **made** sure he wouldn't get **talked** to again.
Voice 1:   **Bully** boy, bully girl, **how** did it end?
Voice 2:   I **thought** they would like me, I **just** want a friend.

You're a **sad**, sad child – you **gotta** lotta trouble.
The **way** you carry on, you're only **making** it double.
Gotta **head** full of anger and a **heart** full of hurt.
Someone's gonna pay for shoving **you** in the dirt.
You **pick** on the ones who never **did** you any wrong,
But **that** won't solve your problem – it'll **just** go on and on.

Chorus

You're a **sad**, sad child with **so** much to prove.
Your **friends**'ll give you aggro if you **don't** stay in the groove.
You're a **puppet** that they play with, doing **every**thing they say,
They **make** you do their dirty work and **then** they run away.
If **that's** the way you keep your friends, of **this** you can be sure,
You'll **end** up much more lonely than you've **ever** been before.

© Anita Haigh 1993

ELDER SON RAP

Key: A
Themes: Fairness, Parables
Based on: Luke 15:25–32 (The parable of the lost son)

Words in **bold** indicate first beat in the bar. Words in CAPITALS said by chorus of voices.

I was **on** my way back home from **work**ing on the LAND
When I **heard** the sound of singing and the **rhythm** of a BAND.
So I **checked** out with a servant – 'Hey, my **man**, what's goin' DOWN?'
He **said**, 'They're celebratin' 'COS YOUR **BRO'S** BACK SAFE AND SOUND.'
Now **I** got really mad, yeah, in **fact**, I was STEAMIN'.
I **couldn't** understand it – I **thought** I must be DREAMIN'.
No **way** was I rejoicin' over **what** that kid had DONE.
My **Dad** came out and asked me, 'SO WHAT'S **GRIEVIN'** YOU, MY SON?'

Chorus
I've been **graftin'**, I've been workin' MY **FINGERS** TO THE BONE,
I've been **dutiful** and faithful, NEVER **RAN** AWAY FROM HOME,
But **what** is my reward for the **LOY**ALTY I'VE SHOWN?
WELL, IT **DON'T** SEEM FAIR TO **ME** — HUH!!

'All these **years** I have worked hard for you, com**pleted** every TASK,
Never **disobeyed** your orders, always **done** as you have ASKED.
And **how** have you repaid me for **all** my toil and SWEAT?
Wasted **money** on that scum WHEN HE'S **UP** TO HERE IN DEBT!

Not one **dime** have you spent cele**bratin'** my hard
WORK,

Yet you **gladly** throw a party for that **selfish** little JERK!

He has **squandered** all your money on **women** and on
WINE,

And you **give** him rings and clothing and RE**PAY** HIM
FOR HIS CRIME!'

Chorus

But my **father** turned and faced me and his **eyes** were
filled with TEARS,

'My **son**, I know how faithful you have **been** these many
YEARS.

You are always with me, every**thing** I have is YOURS,

But you **never** thought to ask me – YOU'RE TOO
BUSY WITH YOUR CHORES!

I'm not your boss – I'm your **father**, you're my SON

So **why** d'you think I'll love you only **if** your work is
DONE?

Your **brother**, he was dead and is **now** alive AGAIN.

He was **lost** and now is found – SHOULD I **NOT** BE
GLAD HE CAME?'

© Anita Haigh 1993

FAST FOOD
a dramatised reading

Key: U
Themes: Faith, Miracles
Based on: Matthew 14:13–21; Mark 6:30–44; Luke 9:10–17; John 6:1–13 (Jesus feeds a great crowd)

Read to a definite rhythm. Best done by four readers, to give the effect of a production line. Last line said after slight pause and not in rhythm, for emphasis.

1:   Fast food
2:   In the oven
3:   Press a switch
4:   Microwave

1:   Quick service
2:   Have a burger
3:   In a bun
4:   With a Coke

1:   Need a bite
2:   While U wait
3:   Get a pizza
4:   On a plate

1:   Five thousand
2:   Needing feeding
3:   Sit them down
4:   On the grass

1:   Five loaves
2:   Two fish
3:   Feed them all
4:   Are you mad?!

1:	Eyes raised
2:	To the heavens
3:	Ask for blessing
4:	On the food

1:	Break the bread
2:	Hand it out
3:	Some left over
4:	Are you sure?

1:	Fast food
2:	Fish 'n' bread
3:	Faith 'n' action
4:	(*Pause*) Nuff said?

From an original idea by Karen Hall 1995
Adapted by Anita Haigh 1996

FOLLOW ME
a poem

Key: U
Themes: Peer pressure, Role models
Based on: Matthew 9:9–13; Mark 2:13–17; Luke 5:27–32
(Jesus Calls Matthew/Levi, Jesus teaches that we should be transformed by God and not conform to others)

Follow me and do as I say.
    Talk as I talk – yeah! that's the way!
If you wanna have status, be in with the crowd,
If you wanna be noticed and made to feel proud,
Then follow me and do as I dare.
    Walk as I walk and wear what I wear.
If you wanna be someone, if you wanna look cool
If you wanna be wanted, then don't be a fool!
Just follow me and think as I think,
    Want what I want and drink what I drink,
Like what I like, hate what I hate,
    Choose what I choose – don't hesitate!
Smoke like I smoke and swear like I swear,
    Buy what I sell – if not, beware!
If you stay as you and think for yourself,
    Make up your mind – you'll be left on the shelf!
So don't analyse it, just swim with the tide.
Follow me, follow me, follow me!

© Anita Haigh 1995

FOLLOW THE MAKER'S INSTRUCTIONS
a sketch

Key: L
Theme: Parables
Based on: Matthew 7:24–27; Luke 6:46–49 (The parable of the two house builders)

Props

2 mixing bowls, 2 wooden spoons, 2 tablespoons, 4 sandwich tins, 2 cookery aprons, 2 sieves, flour, eggs, sugar, marg/butter, chocolate powder, pickle, a chocolate cake, a sandwich tin containing a disaster of a cake!!

Characters

The narrator
Mrs Elsie Bunn, the teacher
Sally, a pupil
Beryl, another pupil
(If the pupils are boys, have Cedric the Sensible and Rodney the Ridiculous instead of Sally and Beryl)

Narrator: It's second lesson at (*school name*) High School and Mrs Elsie Bunn is giving Year 9 a cookery lesson.

Mrs Bunn: Now everyone, I want you to listen very carefully, I shall say this only once. I am going to show you how to make a Victoria Sandwich. Beryl! Face this way! You are not going to learn what to do by staring at Malcolm's left ear! Right.

Well, you take 150 grams of butter and 150 grams of castor sugar and cream them together with a wooden spoon until light and fluffy... Beryl, if you don't pay attention I'll be creaming you until you're light and fluffy! Now where was I? Oh yes. Then make a well in the centre of the mixture and add a beaten egg with one tablespoon of sifted self-raising flour. Mix, adding some more flour, then add the second beaten egg. Continue beating in the flour until all 300 grams have been used up. Then add one heaped tablespoon of chocolate powder to give it that rich dark taste, and beat well for about two minutes. Then divide the mixture evenly between two lightly greased sandwich tins and put into a preheated oven at 180°C for about 25-30 minutes until a rich, dark brown. Right, got that? OK then, off you go…

Narrator: Five minutes later…

Sally: You're supposed to weigh the sugar first, you dummy! That's more like 250 grams than 150!

Beryl: Oh shut up, Miss Know-All. I've made cakes for years at home and no one's complained yet.

Sally: Probably because their jaws are concreted together!

Beryl: My mum just bungs everything in together. She don't bother weighing things. Says it's a waste of time… Now what came next? Make a well and add a sifted egg with 300 grams of flour. Keep using all the eggs until the carton is empty…

Sally: (*Stifling a gasp*) Beryl Blockhead, what are you doing?

Beryl: Mind your own business. I can make a Hysteria Sandwich just like anyone else.

Sally: Like NO ONE else!!

Beryl: What did she say next? Something to give it a rich, dark taste… hmm… oh this will do. Pickle'll definitely give it a dark, spicy flavour anyhow. And now bung it in a tin and shove it in the oven at 280°C for … umm … five minutes, wasn't it? … I'll show that Sally…

Narrator: Thirty minutes later, Mrs Bunn inspects their efforts…

Mrs Bunn: Right. OK, girls, I'd like to mark your finished assignments. Sally?

(Mrs Bunn holds up plate with successful chocolate cake.)

Mrs Bunn: Oh yes! Beautiful texture and not too much chocolate. Well done! An 'A', I think. Now, Beryl, let me have a looo...

(Mrs Bunn holds up something resembling pig swill on a plate.)

Mrs Bunn: What on earth is this? I asked you to make a Victoria Sandwich not a mud pie. I've a good mind to make you eat it! When WILL you learn to follow instructions?!

FORGIVING OR FORGETTING?
a poem

Key: A
Theme: Forgiveness
Based on: Matthew 18:21–35 (The parable of the unforgiving servant)

Can be read by one person, or two people reading alternate lines.

Are you forgiving?
  Or are you for getting?
Getting revenge,
  Getting it straight,
Getting the boot in
  At the school gate?
An eye for an eye,
  A tooth for a tooth,
Well, that's just a lie,
  Let me tell you the truth.
When you mess it up,
When you get it wrong,
When you make mistakes
  And the pressure is on,
What will you want
  From the one that you've hurt?
The offer of peace,
  Or your nose in the dirt?
So are you forgiving?
  Or are you forgetting?
Forgetting your faults,
Forgetting your temper,
Forgetting your rudeness?
  Well, it's time to remember!
To learn from mistakes
  Is a good way to live,
And mercy will come
  To those who forgive.

© Anita Haigh 1995

12 HEART, SOUL & MIND
a sketch

Key: A
Theme: Love, the greatest commandment
Based on: Matthew 22:34–40; Mark 12:28–34; Luke 10:25–28

Props
None required

Characters
A narrator and 2 others

Narrator stands centre stage, Persons 1 and 2 stand on either side of Narrator.

Narrator: One day, a teacher of the law came and asked Jesus...

Person 1: (*Posh voice*) So, tell me – what is the most important law?

Narrator: And Jesus answered, 'To love the Lord your God...'

Person 2: I know all about love! Have you seen that... (*current teen idol*)? He's gorgeous, he is!

Person 1: No, I know all about love; I got fifty Valentine cards from my boyfriend!

Narrator: No, no! That's not what I mean. Jesus said, 'To love the Lord your God with all your heart...'

Person 1: I know about hearts – I've done it in science. There are four chambers – two ventricles and two atriums...

Narrator: Shut up!

Person 2: Yeah, shut up! I know all about hearts. There's this really good card game – you've got to get the ace of hearts to win...
(*Narrator and Person 1 yawn, looking bored.*)

Narrator: No, no! Listen! Jesus said, 'Love the Lord your God with all your heart, all your soul...

Person 1: I know about soles - I've got two soles, one on my right foot (*Lifts foot to show*) and one on my left...

Person 2: No, no! I can tell you what soul is... (*Sings like James Brown*) 'Ow! I feel good!'...

Narrator: Fine! But I don't mean that kind of soul. Jesus said, 'Love the Lord your God with all your heart, all your soul, all your mind...

Person 1: Mined? I know all about that! Coal's mined, tin's mined and even diamonds are...

Person 2: No, you idiot! Mind! You know, what you are completely out of, and what I am about to give you a piece of...

Narrator: Honestly, you two! Will you both just listen! Now, where was I? Oh yes! 'Love the Lord your God with all your heart, all your soul, all your mind, and love your neighbour... .
(*Person 1 and Person 2 sing 'Neighbours' theme tune.*)

Narrator: (*Shouts over the top*) '...Love your neighbour as yourself. And that's how Jesus answered the law expert's question.

13 HYPOCRISY IS...
a short sketch for two readers

Key: U
Theme: Boasting, Hypocrisy
Based on: Matthew 6:1–4 (Jesus' teaching on hypocrisy)

1: Hypocrisy is pretending to be something you're not...

2: Like when you start talking different in front of your mates, and say words like...

1: (*Interrupts quickly*) Hypocrisy is telling someone to do something when you're not prepared to do it yourself.

2: Like when you tell ME to take the dog for a walk, and then go mad when it does a wee on the carpet!

1: (*Ignores 2*) Hypocrisy is when your actions don't match your words.

2: Like when you're being friendly to (*girl's/boy's name as appropriate*) and then slag them off behind their back!

1: (*Continues to ignore 2*) Hypocrisy is finding fault with someone for something that is your own greatest failing. (*Looks accusingly at 2.*)

2: (*To audience*) And (s)he says I'm two-faced!

1: (*Glares at 2*) Hypocrisy is blowing your own trumpet when you've only done your duty.

2: Well then, you'd make up for the entire brass section of an orchestra, wouldn't you? (*Laughs*)

1: (*Dramatically*) Hypocrisy is staging your own encore by making a performance out of doing good. (*Looks smug.*)

2: (*Faces 1*) And hypocrites award themselves Oscars — but that's all the reward they'll ever get.
(*Both freeze.*)

From an original idea by Hannah Jowett 1995
Adapted by Anita Haigh 1996

I'VE GOT MY RIGHTS
a dramatic poem for 3 people

Key: A
Themes: Accountability, Parables, Respect for others, Rights and responsibilities, Selfishness
Based on: Matthew 25:14–30; Luke 19:11–27 (The parable of the three servants)

1: I've got my right
2: My right to speak
3: My right to free expression
All: And so I'll call you what I like
1: To let off my aggression

1: I've got my right
2: My right to choose
3: My right to make decisions
All: And so I'll do just as I please
1: I don't need your permission

1: I've got my right
2: My right to think
3: My right to my religion
All: And truth is what is true for me
1: I don't need your opinion

1: I've got my right
2: My right to live
3: To play life by my game
All: But if I really mess it up
1: It's you that I will blame

© Anita Haigh 1994

15 LOVE IN THE TWENTY-FIRST CENTURY
a monologue

Key: L
Theme: Love, the greatest commandment
Based on: 1 Corinthians 13; Matthew 22:35–40; Mark 12:28–31, Luke 10:25–28

If I speak French so well that I'm mistaken for... (*current French President's name*)
   But have not love
I am only a stuck record on a DJ's turntable.

If I know more about the World Cup than you
And have the faith to believe that one day England will qualify
   But have not love
Then I am nothing.

If I give my monthly pocket money to Guide Dogs for the Blind
And surrender my body to the effects of pollution
   But have not love
I gain nothing.

Love is patient with parents when they say, 'Where do you think you're going?'
   And 'You're not going out dressed like that!'

Love is kind to little brothers who pinch your favourite CDs without asking
   And never give you them back.

Love does not boast that your new trainers cost 80 quid.

It is not proud of how good looking it is.

It is not rude in McDonald's when your hamburger arrives
stone cold
And half an hour late!

It is not self-seeking when somebody pats you on the back
And tells you how nice you are.

It is not easily angered by people who won't listen to you
And always think they know best.

Love keeps no records of times your heart is broken.

Love never fails.

© Hannah Jowett 1992

16 THE LOVE OF MONEY
a monologue

Key: U
Themes: Greed, Selfishness, Wealth
Based on: Matthew 6:19–24; Luke 12:33–34 (The sermon on the mount)

How money can be used to exploit others in order to gain power.

In the beginning, people created the market.

When stomachs were empty and hunger hovered over the faces of the people, they came to the market to buy their goods, each according to their needs.

Then the people said, 'Let there be shops.' And there were.

People saw that the shops were profitable. So they created money with which to buy the goods, and divided the different goods into different kinds of shop.

People named these shops 'The Butcher', 'The Baker', 'The Candlestick-maker'.

Evening passed and morning came – the next day.

Then some people said, 'Let there be something to divide the types of shop into two groups.'

So they made High-class Shops and Other Shops. They named the High-class Shops 'The Delicatessen', 'The Patisserie' and 'Harrods'.

And they created different kinds of money to spend in these shops, each according to their wants. They named this money 'Access', 'Visa' and 'American Express'.

And some people saw that it was profitable. Evening passed and morning came – the next day.

Then some people said, 'Let all the shops be gathered together under one roof, so that many shoppers will appear.' And it happened.

People named this gathering 'The Shopping Complex', and the shoppers' cars gathered in the extensive car parks.

Then some people said, 'Let there be lights to decorate the ceilings, fountains in the walkways and food malls selling fast food full of monosodium glutamate. And let there be Lazer Quest, Ten-Pin Bowling and a Multi-Screen Cinema. And there were.

And some people saw that it was profitable. Evening passed and morning came – the next day.

Then some people said, 'Let there be 'Instant Free Credit' and 'Buy Now – Pay Later' options. Let there be door-to-door sales staff and telesales staff'. And there were.

Some people trained them, saying 'Go forth and sell. Fill your pockets, and let consumers grow in number upon the face of the earth.'

And some people saw that it was profitable. Evening passed and morning came – the next day.

Then some people said, 'Let there be two bright attractions – the greater one to rule the day, and the lesser one to rule the night'.

They named the greater one 'The National Lottery' and the lesser one 'The Cable TV Shopping Directory'. And soon newsagents and supermarkets were teeming with shoppers wanting to buy lottery tickets every Saturday afternoon.

And some people saw that it was profitable. Evening passed, and morning came – the next day.

Then some people said, 'Let us make Money Markets. Let them be in our own image and likeness. Let them rule over all markets, the economy, the environment, development programmes, and over every creature that lives upon the face of the earth.'

So they made Money Markets; Stocks and Shares, The International Monetary Fund, and High Interest Loans, saying, 'Fill the earth and be its master.'

And some people saw that it was very profitable. And they bowed down and worshipped.

17 THE MAN WHO WALKS ON WATER
a rap

Key: L
Themes: Faith, Fear, Jesus' authority, Miracles
Based on: Matthew 14:22–33; Mark 6:45–50; John 6:16–21

Words in **bold** indicate first beat of the bar. Words in CAPITALS said by a chorus of voices.

Yo! listen up and **gimme** some ATTENTION
'Cos **what** I gotta say can give your **life** a new DIMENSION!
Do **people** let you down? Do you **know** who can be TRUSTED?
Are you **scared** of letting go in case your **HOPE** GETS BUSTED?
Can you say your life is **goin'** like it OUGHTA?
THEN **TAKE** A CLOSER LOOK AT THE **MAN** WHO WALKS ON WATER!

Jesus had been talkin' with some **people** all DAY
And **after** he had split the scene, well, **HE** WENT OFF TO PRAY
He **told** his friends to take a boat and **sail** across the LAKE
But **soon** they all were thinkin' THAT **THIS** WAS A MISTAKE!

The **wind** began to blow and the **waves** grew really WILD
AND **EVERY**BODY IN THE BOAT WAS **WAILING** LIKE A CHILD!

But **Jesus** had been watchin' – he **knew** the SITUATION
And **when** he walked across the waves, HE **CAUSED** A
GREAT SENSATION!
As he came toward them, they **all** began to SCREAM
They **hollered**, 'It's a spook! IT'S TOO **BAD** TO BE A
DREAM!'
'Hey **guys!** Come on! There's no **need** to scream 'n'
SHOUT!
IT'S **ME!**' JESUS SAID, 'AND I'M **HERE** TO HELP
YOU OUT!'

Peter spoke up, 'If **what** you say is TRUE
Then **get** me walkin' water – **JUST** THE WAY YOU
DO!'
'Come **on!**' said Jesus, so **Peter** quit the CREW
But **when** he saw the breakers, HE **STARTED** SINKIN'
THROUGH
As he sank down under, he **yelled**, I'm gonna DROWN!'
BUT **JESUS** GRABBED HIM, SAYIN', 'D'YA **THINK**
I'D LET YOU DOWN?'

The **crew** were all in shock when the **two** got in the
BOAT
They **couldn't** figure out how **THEY** WERE STILL
AFLOAT!
But **now** the storm had gone, they **knew** without a
DOUBT
That **this** was the Messiah – THEY'D **FINALLY**
WORKED IT OUT!
So **when** you feel afraid, and your **courage** starts to FALTER
THEN **TAKE** A CLOSER LOOK AT THE **MAN**
WHO WALKS ON WATER

18 MARCH FOR JUSTICE
a chant

Key: L
Themes: Fairness, Justice
Based on: Luke 4:16–19 (The call to justice, Jesus' mission as prophesied in Isaiah 61:1–2)

In the style of a US army chant. The leader chants a line and the audience all repeat it. Can be done to the stomp of marching feet!

Some kids find a car to nick
    As a joke it's pretty sick
As they wreck it, they all cheer
    Owners watching shed a tear

Two men working night and day
    They've got lots of bills to pay
One of them has got the sack
    Just because his skin is black

Bullies find a new victim
    Now they'll make life hell for him
They all thought he was a weed
    Now there's one less mouth to feed

Justice always seem so weak
    We need someone new to speak
To defend the weak and lame
    Jesus said, 'That's why I came'

© Andrew Smith 1995

MERCY TRIUMPHS OVER JUDGEMENT
a sketch

19

Key: U
Theme: Judgementalism
Based on: Luke 7:36–50 (A woman anoints Jesus' feet)

Props
Bibles

Characters
Vicar
Woman 1
Woman 2
Extras as parishioners

Scene
St Swithin's church service. The Vicar is about to preach.
Two women sit together in the pew, holding their Bibles
open.

Vicar: This morning we shall consider the account in
Luke's Gospel of the sinful woman who
anointed Jesus… (*Vicar freezes.*)

Woman 1: (*Nudges friend*) 'Ere! See 'er? She was 'ere last
Sunday morning too. Works at the Bingo Hall.
A right den of iniquity, that is! And she sang all
the 'ymns too!

Woman 2: 'ypocrite!

Woman 1: And did you see 'er praying last week? On 'er
knees, cryin', with 'er arms in the air while we
were supposed to be standing and greeting each
other with the Peace.

Woman 2: Exhibitionist!

Woman 1: And did you notice what she put in the collection plate? Well, she opened 'er 'andbag and
took out a bottle of Yves Saint Laurent Rive
Gauche … and sprayed some in the plate!

Woman 2: Never!

Woman 1: Then she put the 'ole bottle in!

Woman 2: Outrageous!

Woman 1: I mean, what a waste of good perfume, eh?

Woman 2: Too right!

Woman 1: You'd think with some of the little flutters she probably has at work during her tea breaks, that she'd come up with some 'ard cash! Well, wouldn't ya?

Woman 2: Exactly!

Woman 1: Our Sharon met 'er in the Co-op last Thursday, and do you know what she told 'er? She said she felt liberated!

Woman 2: Oh?

Woman 1: Too liberated, if you ask me. I mean, just look at the length of that skirt she's wearin'!

Woman 2: Indecent!

Woman 1: A new woman, she said, released from 'er past, she said.

Woman 2: What nonsense!

Woman 1: It's disgraceful, that's what it is! I don't know … this church is going to the dogs!

Vicar: And Jesus concluded, 'I tell you her many sins have been forgiven – for she loved much. But he who has been forgiven little, loves little.' Amen. Let us say the response together.

All: May the words of my mouth and the meditation of my heart be pleasing in your sight, O Lord, my Rock and my Redeemer.

THE MOBILE CHIPPY & BURGER BAR ASSOCIATION
a monologue

Key: U
Themes: Jesus' authority, Miracles
Based on: Matthew 14:13–21; Mark 6:30–44; Luke 9:10–17; John 6:1–13 (Jesus feeds a great crowd)

Fellow members, I am pleased to see such a good turn-out at today's meeting of the Mobile Chippy and Burger Bar Association. As you know, our Association has been growing in recent years and we have welcomed many into our group. In the last month two new members – Bartholemew's Burgers and Freda's Fry-Up have joined our Association.

But all is not well, fellow members. I have heard deeply disturbing news from a town not far from here.

Now you know that I admire hard work. You know that I am a strong supporter of free enterprise, of a competitive market and a good business plan. But, friends, we must act when our businesses are challenged by someone who is not using the same rule book. We are all willing to compete on a level playing field, but we are now threatened by one who intends to ruin our livelihoods by unfair trade.

Friends, I refer to the incident at Bethsaida. According to my sources a man there was able to provide ready meals for 5,000, I repeat 5,000 people at one sitting. This he seemed to do at very short notice.

Now, we in the trade know that this is not possible. A booking for 5,000 would take months to prepare. Friends, how can we compete with someone who is totally bypassing the stipulations and regulations laid down by our Association? This sort of thing will surely take trade away from the lake-side burger bars and the mobile village chippies.

Do any of you have a supplier who can deliver at a moment's notice? No! We must find out who this man's supplier is!

Some of you will have also heard the rumour that this man supplied all these meals from only five loaves of bread and two fish. I find this extremely worrying. We can compete on equal terms, but this is unfair trading in the extreme. How does he manage to scale down his fish supplies like this?

(*As if responding to a comment from front row.*) What do you mean he made no profit – he gave the meals free of charge? He ignored our Statutory Pricing Policy!

Join with me now, members. We must take action to stamp out this blatant attack on our businesses before this sort of thing takes hold and we are robbed of our bread and butter! We must seek out this man and insist he trade within the regulations now!

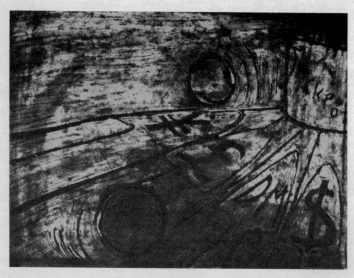

MODERN PARABLE OF THE GOOD SAMARITAN
a poem

Key: A
Themes: Compassion, Parables, Responsibility
Based on: Luke 10:25–37 (The parable of the good Samaritan)

Characters
Mr & Mrs McKenzie
Scottie McKenzie
Extras for rival fans
United fan
Old Sunderland fan
Or one person can recite entire poem, miming all the parts.

Words in **bold** can be replaced with names, teams, colours appropriate to your local situation. Dramatise the poem using appropriate team strips, etc.

At a soccer match down at **Roker**
Noted for punch-ups and brawls,
Mr & Mrs McKenzie   (*Enter McKenzie Family.*)
Took young Scottie to watch the football.

Sunderland were playing **Newcastle**,
And as the team came into view,
'Up with the **Geordies**', yelled Scottie,
'Get in! Show 'em what you can do!'   (*Scottie jumps up and down.*)

The whistle blew - the game had begun.
The crowd shouted and roared.
Then up the sidelines came… (*name of current striker*)
Kicked the ball – and yes! He scored!   (*Family all cheer.*)

49

The **Sunderland** fans weren't too happy,
And soon the scuffles began.
'Down with the **Maccums**!' yelled Scottie.   (*Scottie shakes his fist.*)

His father said, 'Shut up, young man.'   (*Mr McKenzie looks around nervously.*)

'You'll have them doing us over
If they hear you shouting like that!'
And just at that very moment
They were surrounded by **red and white** hats. (*Enter rival fans looking menacing.*)

'Oh blimey!' cried Mr McKenzie,
While his wife went into a faint.   (*Mrs McKenzie swoons.*)
'Which of you's insulting our team like?'
Scottie just smiled like a saint.   (*Scottie makes cheesy grin.*)

The Sunderland fans grabbed young Scottie   (*Rival fans surround Scottie and drag him to one side.*)
And disappeared into the crowd.
They gave him a bit of a dusting
And left him in a heap on the ground.   (*Rival fans exit leaving Scottie on the ground.
Meanwhile Mr McKenzie tries to revive Mrs McKenzie.*)

A **United** supporter walked past him   (*Enter United fan, sees Scottie and looks scared.*)
But was too scared to help the poor lad.
The **red and white** hats made him dizzy,
And his stomach felt really quite bad   (*United fan exits clutching stomach.*)

His mum was still in hysterics,   (*Mrs McKenzie screams.*)
And his dad had gone for a beer.   (*Exit Mr McKenzie.*)
He said it would strengthen his nerve,
But it was really out of cold fear.

Then up came an old **Sunderland** fan,   (*Enter old man.*)
Saw the boy all muddy and sore.
He felt right sorry for young Scottie
And picked him up off the floor.   (*Old man helps
                                                                    Scottie to his feet.*)

He gave him a drink from his hip flask   (*Old man mimes
                                                                 helping Scottie.*)

And wiped the mud from his face.
'Where's your folks?' asked the old man,
'Can't leave you alone in this place.'

At long last came the grand reunion   (*Enter Mr & Mrs
                                                                          McKenzie.*)

With mother still blowing her nose,   (*Mrs McKenzie
                                                    blows her nose in a crumpled hanky.*)

And Dad on his third pint of Guinness,
Just as the match had come to a close.

'A three-all draw,' said the announcer
Amid the boos and the cheers.   (*Exit old man.*)
'Well, the **Maccums** aren't all bad,' said Scottie,
But the kind old man had disappeared.

22 MOUTH ALMIGHTY
a poem

Key: U
Themes: Bullying, Respect for others
Based on: Matthew 5:21–22; 12:33–37; Luke 6:43–45
(The sermon on the mount)

Said assertively.

Don't be a Mouth Almighty.
It isn't very nice.
Before you say a single word, my friend,
You just think twice.

Some people call the mouth 'a gob'
Because it's full of spit
And venom-coated words that spew
So easily from it.

Some people call the mouth 'a trap'.
It takes you by surprise
And gets you in a corner where
It cuts you down to size.

Some people call the mouth 'a hole'
Like the Black Hole of Calcutta,
Full of filth, death and disease,
The language of the gutter.

Some call it 'the kisser'.
Now there's a clever twist!
A charming term that boxers use
For where they punch their fist!

The French call it 'la bouche'
And the Spanish say 'la bocca',
But the mouth in any language
Can be guaranteed to shock ya … So—

Don't be a Mouth Almighty.
Be careful what you say
Because you might just have to eat
Those very words one day.

23 OUTCAST
a poem

Key: U
Themes: Fairness, Justice, Parables, Rejection, Respect for others
Based on: Matthew 25:31–46 (The parable of the sheep and goats)

Did you hear the news today?
He's infected with a killer disease
    Words stick in his throat
What can he say?
What can he say as he feels himself
    Grow weaker day by day?

Did you see his face today?
Did you hear his family slam the door?
    'We don't have a brother anymore.'
In shock and pain
    They are torn apart.
They can't bear the pain
    Of the son they ignore.

I saw an outcast today.
He walks carefully, his hair's turned grey.
He smiles to his friends—
    Their response is cold.
He waves to his neighbours—
    They turn their heads and cross the road.

Old men hurl insults,
    Young men throw stones.
People won't enter these tragic homes.
God sees a broken man standing alone.
    He picks this man up and carries him home.

© Helen Anderson 1996

THE PARABLE OF NORBUTT AND CEDRIC
a sketch

Key: L
Theme: Parables
Based on: Matthew 7:24–27; Luke 6:46–49 (The parable of the two house builders)

Props

Fizzy drink cans and crisp packets
Boxes of 'fireworks'
2 tables
A 'Firework Code' book
A sheet of paper
A Beano comic and a toy rabbit
2 long tapers

Characters

Norbutt
Cedric
Narrator
6 Extras to play their friends

Narrator: Introducing Norbutt and Cedric.
(*Norbutt and Cedric bow.*)
Narrator: They were next door neighbours.
N & C: (*Sing 'Neighbours' theme tune.*)
Narrator: Shhhh—stop interrupting!! They lived in Foundation Street. Every day they would get up at 7.30 (*Norbutt and Cedric yawn and stretch*), eat their All-Bran… (*They mime eating.*)
N & C: (*Say in unison*) Keeps ya nice and regular!
Narrator: Go to work…
(*Norbutt and Cedric stand and mime clutching their briefcase and swaying on a bus/train.*)
Narrator: …at the office.
N & C: Type, type, dring, dring! Type, type, dring, dring! (*Mime typing and answering the phone.*)
Narrator: Their day would end after tea, watching the news. (*Norbutt and Cedric sit watching TV.*)
Norbutt: Boing! Boing!
Cedric: The News at Ten with… (*any current newsreader*).
Narrator: And then it was off to bed.

	(*Norbutt and Cedric snore on the 'beds'.*)
Narrator:	And the next day it would be just the same. They would wake up…
	(*Norbutt and Cedric yawn and stretch.*)
Narrator:	Eat breakfast…
N & C:	Keeps you nice and regular! (*Mime eating.*)
Narrator:	Go to work…
	(*Norbutt and Cedric clutch clutch, sway, sway.*)
Narrator:	…At the office.
N & C:	Type, type, dring, dring! Type, type, dring, dring! (*Mime typing and answering the phone.*)
Narrator:	Watch the news…
N & C:	Boing, boing, the News at Ten with… (*current newsreader.*)
Narrator:	Off to bed.
	(*Norbutt and Cedric snore.*)
Narrator:	In fact, every day it was just the same. (*Norbutt and Cedric repeat their words and actions – 'Get up at 7.30' … 'off to bed' – three times, getting faster each time.*)
Narrator:	But one particular day it was different. It was… (*any special occasion, eg bonfire night*) and Cedric had an idea (*Cedric's face lights up*) and Norbutt had an idea (*Norbutt's face lights up*).
N & C:	(*In unison*) I know! Tonight is… (*any special occasion*). I'm going to have a Firework Party!
Narrator:	So they began to prepare. First, they rang all their friends.
N & C:	(*In unison*) Dring, dring! (*Mime holding the phone.*) Do you wanna come to a party?
Narrator:	Then they bought some fizzy pop and crisps. (*Norbutt and Cedric each put coke cans and crisps on their table.*) They collected some wood and made their bonfires.(*Norbutt and Cedric make wood piles.*) And each bought a box of fireworks. (*Norbutt and Cedric each put box on table.*) Then they sat down and waited for their friends to arrive. Cedric read the Firework Code from cover to cover. (*Cedric reads.*) And Norbutt read

the *Beano* from cover to cover. (*Norbutt reads.*) Cedric bought his pet rabbit inside for safety. (*Cedric puts rabbit on table.*) Norbutt read the *Beano* inside out. (*Norbutt turns pages of comic.*) Cedric got the long tapers ready for lighting the fireworks. (*Cedric puts taper on table.*) Norbutt read the *Beano* upside down (*Norbutt turns comic upside down.*) Cedric went and arranged the fireworks in proper stands at a safe distance from the house. (*Cedric arranges fireworks.*) Norbutt made the *Beano* into an aeroplane (*Norbutt folds comic into paper plane and chucks it.*) Then their friends arrived. (*Six extras come forward, 3 friends for each.*) Soon it was time to light the fireworks. Cedric said…

Cedric: (*Clutching Firework Code*) Stand back! Fireworks can be dangerous! (*Cedric's friends move to a safe distance.*)

Narrator: And Norbutt said…

Norbutt: Do you wanna see my Turbo-Powered Super-Booster Rocket? (*Norbutt's friends move too close to his wood pile.*)

Narrator: Then Cedric lit his firework.
(*Cedric and his friends 'Ooh' and 'Aaah' in wonder.*)

Narrator: Then Norbutt lit his firework … BANG!
(*Norbutt and friends fall down.*)

© Anita Haigh 1996

25 POSTMAN PAT DELIVERS GOOD NEWS
a sketch

Key: A
Theme: Parables
Based on: Matthew 13:1–9; Mark 4:1–9; Luke 8:4–8 (The parable of the sower)

Props

Postman Pat hat (or similar!)
Pat's postbag
4 sealed envelopes containing letters
Outrageous piece of fashionable clothing
A newspaper
A pair of shades
Leather (or other trendy) jacket
A telephone

Characters

Postman Pat
Billy Bovver
Felicity Fickle
Mandy Militant
Wayne Wiseman
Chorus of people to sing 'Postman Pat' theme tune
Trendy Friend

	(*Enter Postman Pat to chorus of theme tune.*)
Narrator:	One morning, a postman called Pat had to deliver a letter to Billy Bovver. Billy was rock hard.
	(*Enter Billy Bovver looking tough. Postman Pat hands letter to Billy who snatches it out of his hand and flexes his muscles.*)
Billy B:	I'm rock hard, all right?! (*Exit Postman Pat hurriedly.*)
Narrator:	Billy read the letter.
Billy B:	(*In a gruff voice*) 'Dear Billy, you're very sure of yourself but don't seem to enjoy life much. How about giving me a call and I'd be glad to show you how to get the most out of life. Love, God. RSVP.'
Narrator:	But Billy was not amused.
Billy B:	I am not amused. Who does this geezer think he is – God or something? Huh? That stuff's for wimps, not rock hard people like me.

(*Billy screws up letter, throws it on floor and exits. Enter Postman Pat to theme tune.*)

Narrator: Pat also delivered a letter to Felicity Fickle who followed fashion fiendishly.

(*Enter Felicity Fickle who talks in 'dumb blonde' accent and giggles a lot.*)

Felicity F: I'm a fashion fiend – look what I bought in Betty's Boutique!

(*She holds up outrageous piece of clothing.*)

Felicity F: Ooh, Mr Postie, a little old letter for little old me? Oooh…

(*Exit Postman Pat hurriedly. Felicity reads letter aloud.*)

Felicity F: 'Dear Fliss…' Ooh! (*Giggles*) .'You don't seem to know what you really want in life. Give me a call and I'll help you sort things out. My outfit's really radical!! Love, God. RSVP.' (*Giggles*) Oooh, isn't he such a cutie! Must ring him sometime. Wonder what that outfit he mentioned looks like? … Now what am I going to wear to this party tonight?…

(*Exit Felicity mumbling about party. Enter Postman Pat to theme tune.*)

Narrator: The next letter was for Mandy Militant. She had very strong views about everything. At least she had very strong views about whatever her friends had very strong views about!

(*Enter Mandy Militant clutching newspaper and waving it in the air.*)

Mandy M: (*Shouts*) Socialist Worker, get your Socialist Worker! Save the seal! Ban the Bomb! Rights for Rodents! Flowers have feelings!

(*Mandy takes letter from Postman Pat who exits hurriedly.*)

Mandy M: What's this? Probably new orders for my next demonstration from Central Control… (*Reads letter aloud*) 'Dear Mandy, you've got very strong views about life, but I'd like to give you a real cause to fight for in life. Call soon. Love, God. RSVP.' Mmm, an interesting cause… (*Shouting*) Join the God Squad! Buy the Bible! Profit from Prayer…

(*Enter Trendy Friend in shades and leather jacket looking 'cool'. Interrupts Militant Mandy.*)

Trendy F: Hey, hey, hey! We don't want no agitation, persuasion or misinformation. Popular opinion is our religion. Believing just ain't cool! (*Clicks fingers.*)

(*Mandy shrugs shoulders, screws up letter and continues shouting. Trendy Friend exits.*)

Militant M: Conformers unite! Go with the flow! Swim with the tide!…

(*Enter Postman Pat to theme tune.*)

Narrator Now Postman Pat's last letter was for Wayne Wiseman. He always thought through everything very carefully.

(*Postman Pat hands Wayne a letter.*)

Wayne W: I wonder who this is from? Now let me see…

(*Postman Pat exits. Wayne opens letter and reads aloud.*)

Wayne W: 'Dear Wayne, I know you think about life's questions carefully. Well, I am a question that I'd like you to think about very carefully. How about calling me for some answers? Love, God. RSVP.' I wonder what he means by that? Well, no harm in finding out. He wouldn't have written if it wasn't important, I suppose… Perhaps I'll give him a call…

(*Wayne goes to phone, dials and waits a short while.*)

Wayne W: Oh, God? That you?… Oh, hello… It's Wayne here. Now about your letter… (*Wayne freezes.*)

RICH YOUNG RULER
a rap

Key: L
Themes: Parables, True security, Wealth
Based on: Luke 18:18–24; Matthew 19:16–24; Mark
10:17–24 (The parable of the rich young ruler)

Words in **bold** indicate first beat in the bar.

Put your hands together, let's **hear** you clap!
Gotta **keep** the beat going, let's **see** you rap!
Gonna **tell** you all a story, so **listen** up good!
'Bout a **Rich** Young Ruler – a **real** cool dude!

Now the **Rich** Young Ruler came to **Jesus** one day.
He said, '**Hey**, Good Teacher! What **would** you say
If I **asked** you how to gain **eternal** life?
I **don't** steal from my neighbour or **cheat** on the wife,
I've **never** lied in court or **killed** anyone,
To my **mother** and my father I'm a **loyal** son.'
But **Jesus** said, 'You gotta **do** something more,
Gotta **sell** all you have and **give** to it to the poor.'

'You'll have **treasure** in heaven for **eternit**y
If you **leave** everything and **follow** me.'
But the **Rich** Young Ruler looked **mighty** sad.
He **couldn't** bear to give away **all** he had.

Jesus **said**, 'Camels pass through a **needle's** eye
More **easy** than the rich get to **heaven** when they die!'
Jesus **said**, 'Camels pass through a **needle's** eye
More **easy** than the rich get to **heaven** when they die!'

© Anita Haigh 1990

27 | THE STORY OF BERTIE BALLOON
a monologue

Key: A
Themes: Parables, True security, Wealth
Based on: Luke 12:16–21 (The parable of the rich fool)

Props
One good quality balloon
A permanent marker pen
A teddy
Some toy money

Can be performed by one person, or by two people with one narrating and one blowing up the balloon. The end should come as a surprise!

Once upon a time Mrs Balloon gave birth to a bouncing baby boy called Bertie. (*Blow up balloon a little.*) He was very cute, with a bald head and blue eyes. (*Draw eyes/mouth, etc.*) Most of the time he spent eating, sleeping, crying AND – filling his nappy. (*Let some air out of the balloon.*) Time went by...

When he was 3 years old, Bertie went to playgroup. (*Blow a little more air into the balloon.*) He was very cute in his designer dungarees. Most of the time he spent sitting in the Wendy house talking to his teddy. (*Hold up teddy.*) Time went by...

When he was 5 years old, Bertie went to primary school. (*Blow balloon a bit larger.*) He was very cute in his new school uniform. Most of the time he was a good boy, BUT – he did head-butt his classmate for pinching his Lion King (*or current Disney hero*) pencil case. (*Hit Narrator on the head with balloon.*) Time went by...

By the time he was 16 and in secondary school (*inflate balloon a bit more*) Bertie was a real cool dude with designer trainers, designer haircuts and designer excuses for not having done his homework. Most of the time he spent eyeing up blue-eyed, blonde Belinda. (*Make balloon 'kiss' female member of audience.*) Time went by...

A few years latter, Bertie married Belinda. *(Inflate balloon a bit more.)* He got a good job earning a lot of dosh BUT – most of the time he was busy wishing he had more. So he spent more and more time at work. Time went by...

Fairly soon, Bertie got a promotion, and earned even more dosh. His wallet grew bigger, his car grew bigger, his house grew bigger AND – so did his head (*inflate balloon more*), so he didn't see much of Belinda. (*Wave money.*)

Some years later, Bertie retired. He had a big house, a big car, a big yacht AND – a big pension. Belinda hoped she would at last see more of Bertie BUT – suddenly time ran out. (*Burst balloon.*)

28

THE STORY OF JULIAN
a short sketch

Key: A
Themes: Accountability, Parables, Responsibility, Selfishness
Based on: Matthew 25:31–46 (The parable of the sheep and goats)

Props
A wastepaper bin full of rubbish
Squash racket
Large cardboard box
Coat and hat

Characters
Narrator, to tell story
Julian
Extra to play the other parts

This is the story of Julian. (*Enter Julian, looking smug.*) Julian was a lad who wanted to live a good life and not get into any trouble. (*Julian nods in agreement.*)

One day he saw a fly dying on the window sill. But he didn't do or say anything – it wasn't his responsibility, was it? (*Julian flicks 'fly' away.*)

The next day he saw a young bird that had fallen out of its nest. But he didn't do or say anything – it wasn't his responsibility, was it? (*Julian looks at 'bird' struggling on the floor and shrugs shoulders.*)

Later, he saw a man chucking rubbish into the street. (*Man empties rubbish at Julian's feet.*) And he saw someone shoplifting in the local sports shop. (*Shoplifter walks quickly past Julian with squash racket stuffed up jumper.*) But he didn't do or say anything – it wasn't his responsibility, was it?

The next day, he saw someone sleeping in a cardboard box. (*Julian walks over to homeless person sitting inside box, then shrugs his shoulders and walks away.*) But he didn't do or say anything – it wasn't his responsibility, was it?

Then the man in front of him at the bus queue (*enter man who stands in front of Julian*) had a heart attack and died. (*Man clutches chest and falls to the floor.*), so Julian got a taxi home instead. (*Julian walks away from dead man and hails taxi.*)

Julian liked to go to the amusement arcades – well, it didn't harm anyone, did it? (*Julian mimes playing on One-Arm Bandit.*) But unfortunately he got addicted (*Julian gambles feverishly*) and started to spend ALL his money there. (*Julian shows empty pockets.*) But his friends didn't do or say anything – it wasn't their responsibility, was it?

He skived work to play the machines, and his boss gave him the sack. (*'Boss' chucks hat and coat at Julian and 'points sternly to door.*) But his friends didn't do or say anything – Julian wasn't much fun any more.

He couldn't pay the rent so he got thrown out of his flat. He went to live at No 3, The Cardboard Box, Railway Arch. (*Box is thrown at Julian who looks miserable.*) But his friends didn't do or say anything – hewas getting embarrassing.

He could no longer afford to buy food. But his friends … lost interest. (*Julian clutches stomach while friend walks by, ignoring him.*)

His clothes got very shabby … and smelly … so his friends … ditched him. (*Julian hangs head in sorrow and shame.*)

He caught a bad chest infection. (*Julian coughs, wheezes and splutters.*) But nobody did or said anything – it wasn't their responsibility, was it?

And then Julian … died. (*Julian falls to floor.*)

© Nick Haigh 1994

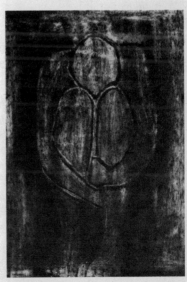

THAT'S NOT FAIR!
a poem

Key: A
Themes: Bullying, Fairness, Respect for others, Responsibility
Based on: Luke 4:16–19 (The call to justice, Jesus' mission as prophesied in Isaiah 61:1–2)

May be read by one reader, or by two readers saying alternate lines. Put emphasis on the last phrase.

When your brother makes a mess and you're made to tidy up,
When the Ref ignores a foul and your team don't win the cup,
When your mate misunderstands you and goes off in a huff,
Well, that's not fair.

When the teacher tells you off when it wasn't you that talked,
And you lend a CD out – and now your whole collec-
tion's walked,
When the umpire says it's 'Out' and you saw that dust of
chalk,
Well, that's not fair.

When someone in your class is treated just like dirt,
Cos they've not got Reebok trainers or a new designer shirt,
When their human-ness is trampled by remarks that really hurt,
Well, that's not fair.

When people are rejected for the colour of their skin,
Or made to feel unwanted for being fat – or thin,
Or judged by their accent, or the house that they live in,
Well, that's not fair.

When people are made prisoners by others' jealousy.
Or treated with injustice, or deprived of dignity.
And it's in our power to act, but we just stand silently.
Then that's not fair — AT ALL.

© Anita Haigh 1996

TIME RAP

Key: L
Themes: Anxiety, Time
Based on: Matthew 6:25–34; Luke 12:22–31 (The sermon on the mount)

Can be performed to a metronome accompaniment! Words in **bold** indicate first beat in the bar. Words in CAPITALS said by chorus of voices.

Tick, tick, **tick**, tick—

Chorus
Seconds, minutes, **hours**, days—
Time is what we're talking **about**.
Days, weeks, **seasons**, years—
Time is what we're talking **about** — YO!

You **wake** up in the morning, brush the **sleep** from your EYES,
Jump into the shower – SEE **HOW** THE TIME FLIES.
No time to eat – **isn't** it a CRIME?
So much to do AND **SO** LITTLE TIME!

Chorus

You **rush** for the bus to **take** you to SCHOOL.
Your **hair's** in a mess – YOU **FEEL** SUCH A FOOL.
You **run** through the gates, but it's **just** gone NINE
And the **teacher** yells at you, 'CAN'T YOU **GET** HERE ON TIME?'

Chorus

First thing this morning, it's the **Maths** EXAM.
Should'na gone out, SHOULD'VE **LISTENED** TO YOUR MAM!
The **questions** are rock – it's **blowing** your MIND!
Better get thinking – IT'S A **RACE** AGAINST TIME!

Chorus

Jesus said, 'See the **birds** of the AIR,
They don't sow or reap – **THEY** DON'T HAVE A
  CARE!
Yet the **Father** feeds them all. Aren't **you** worth more than
  THEY?
Can **worry**, fret 'n' hurry ADD ONE **SECOND** TO
  YOUR DAY?

Chorus

You're **still** so young, got your **whole** life AHEAD.
No time to think about **BEIN'** DEAD!
If you **wanna** live life with **total** peace of MIND
THEN **THINK** ABOUT THE ONE WHO **CREATED**
  ALL OF TIME!

Chorus (*Say last line of chorus three times.*)

Key: L
Themes: Response to God, True security, Wealth
Based on: Luke 19:1–10 (Zacchaeus, the tax collector)

Words in **bold** indicate first beat in the bar.

Now **Zack** collected tax down in **Jericho**.
He was **hated** by the people for **doing** so.
See, he **worked** for the Romans, the **enemies** of the Jews
And he'd **got** mighty wealthy by **collect**ing their dues.

Now **Zack** heard that Jesus was **coming** to town.
He **wanted** to see him **along** with the crowd,
But **he** was so short, not a **thing** could he see,
So he **ran** on ahead and climbed a **sycamore** tree.
As **Jesus** passed by he looked **up** with a smile,
'Hey, **Zack**! Come down! I wanna **stay** with you a while!'
Zack **climbed** down at once – he **felt** a real winner,
But **people** moaned that Jesus was **eating** with a sinner.

By the **end** of the day, they didn't **recognise** Zack
'Cos he **started** to give them all their **money** back.
He gave **half** of all he owned **to** the poor
And to **those** he'd cheated, he **paid** them four times more!

Jesus **said**, 'I've come to **seek** and save the lost.'
Zack **knew** to follow Jesus was **really** worth the cost!
Jesus **said**, 'I've come to **seek** and save the lost
Zack **knew** to follow Jesus was **really** worth the cost!

© Anita Haigh 1990

32 CHRISTMAS RAPPING

Key: A
Theme: Christmas
Based on: Matthew 1:18–25, Luke 1:26–38; 2:1–20

Words in **bold** indicate first beat in the bar. Words in CAPITALS said by chorus of voices.

Listen up you all – I gotta **story** to tell,
Be**ginning** with Mary and the **Angel** Gabriel.
Now **Gabriel** was sent by **God** to hit the Earth,
To **tell** her the news of a **miracle** birth,
That **she** would have a baby, the **Son** of the Most High.
'**OK**, God,' said Mary 'cos she **knew** he wouldn't lie.

Chorus
CHECK IT **OUT**, HUH! **SEE** WHAT IT'S WORTH!
WHAT YA GONNA DO ABOUT THE **MIRACLE**
  BIRTH?
CHECK IT **OUT**, HUH! **SEE** WHAT IT'S WORTH!
WHAT YA GONNA DO ABOUT THE **MIRACLE**
  BIRTH?

When **Joseph** heard that Mary was **gonna** have a baby,
He was most disturbed and he **started** thinking, 'Maybe
I **ought** to leave this woman – they'll **think** the child is
  mine!'
But an **angel** came to tell him that the **baby** was divine,
'Don't **worry**, Joe, be happy! 'Cos **God** has blessed your
  life!'
So **Joseph** said, 'That's cool, man!' and took **Mary** for his
  wife.

Chorus

A **little** later on, the **couple** moseyed down
To **register** their names in **Bethlehem** town.
They **tried** to find a room **where** they both could stay,
But there **wasn't** any spare, so they **slept** out in the hay.
The **only** place they found was a **stable** out the back,
So the **King** of all Creation was **born** down in a shack.

Chorus

Some **shepherds** on a hillside were **in** for quite a shock
When an **angel** came and said, 'Yo dudes!' I'm **gonna** rock
 the flock!
'Cos **there's** a new-born baby who you **guys** should go
 and see,
And **he** is someone special and will **set** the people free!'
They **all** believed the angel – they **didn't** think it odd –
So they **hurried** off to Bethlehem and **found** the Son of
 God.

Chorus

Now **there** are those who think that this **story** isn't true,
That **it's** some kind of fairy-tale that **kids'll** listen to.
But **you'll** find it in the Bible, not **in** a story book,
So **why** not check it out and **take** a closer look?
'Cos the **baby** in the manger – he grew **up** to be a man
And **destroyed** the Devil's
 work – and **that's**
 God's Rescue Plan!

© Anita Haigh 1992

33 LOW-BUDGET NATIVITY PLAY
a short sketch

Key: A
Theme: Christmas
Based on: Matthew 1 & 2; Luke 2; John 14:6 (last line)

Characters
The Angel Gabriel
Mary
One person to play the wise men
One person to play the shepherds
One person to play the animals
The narrator

No props are required. All the characters stand in a line. Words are said in a matter-of-fact, deadpan manner – except the Angel Gabriel who, in contrast, is very melodramatic!

Narrator:	I am the Narrator.
Mary:	I am Mary.
Shepherds:	I am loads of shepherds.
Wise men:	I am the wise men.
Animals:	I am the animals – moo, baa, hee-haw!
Angel Gabriel:	(*Slowly and majestically.*) I am the Angel Gabriel.
Narrator:	And it was at this time, in the land of Galilee, there lived a young woman called Mary.
Mary:	I am Mary.
Narrator:	And there appeared an angel, Gabriel.
Angel Gabriel:	(*Dramatically*) I AM the Angel Gabriel.
Narrator:	And he said…
Angel Gabriel:	Who said?
Narrator:	YOU said.
Angel Gabriel:	Who, me said?
Narrator:	Yes, YOU said.

Angel Gabriel:	What?
Narrator:	You tell me.
Angel Gabriel:	All right.
Narrator:	(*Pause*) Well, go on! SAY IT!
Angel Gabriel:	(*Slowly and majestically*) Hail, Mary! You are the most honoured lady 'cos you will have a baby when the Holy Spirit comes upon you. He will be the Son of the Most High and you will call him Jesus.
Mary:	Pardon?
Angel Gabriel:	(*Impatiently*) You're going to have a baby…
Mary:	All right.
Angel Gabriel:	…He will be God's Son.
Mary:	All right.
Narrator:	Later on, loads of shepherds sat on a hill.
Shepherds:	I am loads of shepherds.
Narrator:	And the Angel Gabriel appeared.
Angel Gabriel:	(*Dramatically*) I AM the Angel Gabriel!
Narrator:	And he said…
Angel Gabriel:	(*Slowly and majestically*) Behold! I bring you great news that a Saviour has been born to you. He is Christ the Lord!
Shepherds:	You what?
Angel Gabriel:	(*Impatiently*) A baby's been born down in a stable…
Shepherds:	All right.
Angel Gabriel:	Go down and see him…
Shepherds:	All right.
Angel Gabriel:	…And do not be afraid.
Shepherds:	All right.
Narrator:	So they went.
Mary:	Hello.
Shepherds:	Hello.
Mary:	Who are you?
Shepherds:	I am loads of shepherds.
Mary:	I am Mary.
Shepherds:	Have you had a baby?
Mary:	Yes. I'm so happy!

Shepherds:	We've come to see him.
Mary:	Why?
Shepherds:	'Cos of that Angel.
Angel Gabriel:	(*Very dramatically*) I AM the Angel Gabriel! (*There is a pause while everyone looks at him.*)
Angel Gabriel:	Sorry…
Shepherds:	He told us about this stable, where animals are kept.
Animals:	I am the animals – moo, baa, hee-haw!
Shepherds:	And here we are.
Mary:	All right.
Shepherds:	And we're so glad.
Mary:	All right.
Shepherds:	And we've bought some sheep as presents.
Mary:	(*In voice like the Philadelphia cheese ad*) Lovely!
Animals:	More animals – moo, baa, hee-haw!
Narrator:	Then some more guests turned up.
Wise Men:	I am the wise men.
Mary:	Hello.
Wise Men:	Hello.
Mary:	Why are you here?
Wise Men:	We followed a star.
Mary:	What, no angel?
Angel Gabriel:	(*Very dramatically*) I AM the Angel Gabriel! (*There is a pause while everyone looks at him again.*)
Angel Gabriel:	Sorry…
Wise Men:	No angel, just a bright star.
Mary:	All right.
Wise Men:	We have brought gifts.
Mary:	All right.
Wise Men:	We have brought gold, incense and myrrh.
Mary:	All right.
Wise Men:	They are for the baby.
Mary:	All right.
	(*They all look at the baby and the presents.*)
Wise Men:	He will be a king.
Mary:	All right.

Wise Men:	We are so honoured.
Shepherds:	We're so glad.
Mary:	I'm so happy.
Animals:	We're so noisy – moo, baa, hee-haw!
Angel Gabriel:	(*Dramatically*) I AM the Angel Gabriel!
Others:	We know, but thank you all the same.
Narrator:	And they all went back home and very little was heard of any of them, except the baby. He grew to be a man who said, 'I am the way, the truth and the life, no one comes to the Father except through me.'

34

MARY'S VISITOR
a sketch

Key: A
Themes: Christmas, Obedience, Response to God
Based on: Luke 1:26–38

Without Mary's trust in God – and her willingness to go through with a mind-boggling, embarrassing and, from our human perspective, utterly incredible plan – we would have no Christ and therefore no Christmas to celebrate.

Props
Housecoat and headscarf
Duster, broom and radio
Small table and chairs
'Drinks cabinet'
Wine/gin bottles and glasses
Yellow Pages directory

Characters
Narrator
Mary
Angel Gabriel
Someone with a Bible

Scene
An ordinary living room with small table and chairs. In a corner is a 'drinks cabinet' holding bottles and glasses.

Narrator: (*Like a Radio 1 DJ*) It's Friday afternoon in downtown Nazareth. At Number 16 Camel Terrace, Mary is busy doing the housework while listening to her favourite Hebrew melodies on Radio Rabbi, the Number One Sound! Little does she know that someone special is winging his way to bring her some rather startling news!
(*Exit Narrator and enter Mary dressed in housecoat and headscarf, holding broom in one hand and radio in the other. She puts radio on table and gives room a sweep with pop music blaring.*)

Mary: Cor, just look at the mess in 'ere! That Joseph! Wish 'e'd leave them blinkin' goats outside!
(*Gabriel appears at the door dressed in white robe,*

sandals and halo, clutching 'Yellow Pages'.)

Gabriel: (*Softly spoken*) Hail, Mary!
(*Mary doesn't hear and carries on sweeping.*)

Gabriel: (*Steps into room and says a bit louder*) Hail, Mary!
(*Mary looks up, but not in Gabriel's direction, so she doesn't see him.*)

Mary: That you, Joseph? (*No reply so she shrugs shoulders and continues sweeping.*)

Gabriel: (*Half shouting*) Hail, Mary!

Mary: (*Looks out of window, shakes head with a puzzled look*) What hail? Don't be so silly, Joseph, it's perfectly sunny outside!

Gabriel: (*Shouts really loud*) HAIL, MARY!!
(*He jumps in front of Mary who screams and drops the duster and broom.*)

Mary: AAAH! Who are you? What're you doin' 'ere? Gave me a dreadful fright...
(*Mary continues to mutter breathlessly with hand on heart. Gabriel switches off radio.*)

Gabriel: (*In refined voice*) Hail, most highly favoured! The Lord is with thee...
(*Mary is confused and looks around fearfully, expecting to see God.*)

Mary: Yer what?

Gabriel: Don't be afraid, Mary. You have found favour with God...
(*Gabriel pauses. He sees this is going to be hard work, so he pushes Mary into a nearby chair.*)

Gabriel: Here, I think you'd better sit down...
(*He pours them both a drink, and Mary gulps it down.*)

Gabriel: You are going to be with child and...

Mary: (*Screams and jumps up*) NOW JUST WATCH IT! Who's been saying things?
(*Gabriel shoves her back into the chair.*)

Gabriel: Calm down, old girl. (*Grandly*) The child will be the Son of the Most High God, and he will be given the throne of his father David...

Mary: David? David? My bloke's name is Joseph!

Gabriel: (*Ignoring her*) He will reign over the house of

	Jacob forever and ever, and his Kingdom will have no end.
Mary:	(*More interested*) Palaces, thrones? And how will this king – this baby – arrive? (*Embarrassed*) I'm … um … I mean. We ain't married yet!
Gabriel:	(*Moves closer to Mary and says dramatically*) The Holy Spirit shall come upon you and the power of the Most High will overshadow you!
	(*He leans over her and she slithers down in her chair, looking very worried.*)
Gabriel:	…So the Holy One born to you will be God's Son, and you will name him… (*Pauses and then says grandly*) Jesus!
Mary:	(*Cackles loudly and slaps Gabriel on the back*) Don't be daft! With a name like that, he won't half get ribbed at school!
	(*She pushes Gabriel out of the way, picks up her broom and duster and carries on cleaning.*)
Mary:	Now a joke's a joke, mate, but I've got loads to do so if you don't mind, 'op it like a little angel. (*Realises pun and cackles*) Like an angel, eh! Geddit? An angel…
	(*Gabriel is not amused. Looking very fed up, he opens 'Yellow Pages'.*)
Gabriel:	I'm sure I've got the right address. V … V … Virgin Atlantic … Virgin Records … Virgin Mary … Mmm… Ah…
	(*He exits, scratching his head with bemused expression.*)
Mary:	(*Still laughing to herself*) Gonna have a baby! What a joke! Jesus too! What a name! … Well I never! …
	(*Exit Mary. Enter Narrator and Someone with a Bible.*)
Narrator:	What a good job Mary wasn't really so busy – and so suspicious of Gabriel and so unsure of God. Otherwise we might never have had a Christmas. Let's hear what really happened.
	(*Someone with a Bible then reads aloud Luke 1:26–38.*)

© Anita Haigh

THE NATIVITY
a sketch

35

Key: A
Theme: Christmas
Based on: Matthew 1 & 2 and Luke 2

Props

Two chairs
A broom
A large, inflatable hammer
A cup of water
Tables laid out like market stalls
Bags of money and coins
A map and a torch

Characters

Mary
Joseph
Angel Gabriel
3 Shepherds
2 Sheep
3 Stallholders
3 Wise Men
Extra Angels
Extra Shepherds
Extra Stallholders
3 Servants

Act 1: The Annunciation

Scene: The house where Mary and Joseph will live when they are married. There are two chairs in the room.

	(*Enter Mary sweeping with the broom.*)
Mary:	(*Calling off-stage*) Joseph! Joseph! Have you finished putting that shelf up yet? (*Sounds of hammering off-stage.*)
Mary:	Well hurry up, we haven't got long to get this place ready before we get married and move in. (*The Angel Gabriel enters and stands behind Mary.*)
Gabriel:	Mary, Mary!
Mary:	(*Not realising who it is*) What is it, Joseph?
Gabriel:	Mary, Mary!
Mary:	(*Still not realising*) Yes, what is it, Joseph? (*Gabriel taps Mary on the shoulder and coughs. Mary jumps, turns round and sees him.*)

Mary:	AAAGH! Who are you? What are you doing in my house? You come near me and I'll give you a taste of me broom. (*She waggles it threateningly at him.*)
Gabriel:	Mary, relax. I'm the Angel Gabriel, sent to you by God, so don't be afraid. The Lord is with you and you are going to have a child called Jesus.
Mary:	Oh my goodness! (*She collapses into a chair.*)
Gabriel:	Your son is going to be great. He will be called the Son of the Most High. He will reign for ever and his Kingdom will never end.
Mary:	But, but, but … I mean, we're not married or anything.
Gabriel:	Don't worry. It is through God's power that you will have a baby, and he will be called the Son of God.
Mary:	Well, I never did! But God is great, so may it be as you have said.
Gabriel:	I'll be on my way then. Cheerio!
Mary:	Goodbye!
Gabriel:	(*Pauses*) Oh … Congratulations on having a baby. (*He exits.*)
Mary:	(*Calling off-stage*) Joseph! Joseph! Stop all that hammering and come in here. (*Hammering sounds cease and Joseph enters, carrying a large inflatable hammer.*)
Joseph:	Here I am Mary. What's the matter?
Mary:	Joseph, I'm going to have a baby. (*Joseph falls over in a dead faint.*)
Mary:	(*Trying to wake him up*) Joseph! Get up, get up! Oh good grief! Well, there's only one thing for it… (*She gets a cup of water and throws it over him. He wakes up with a start.*)
Joseph:	Where? What? When? Who? … Oh Mary, there you are. I had a dreadful dream. I dreamt that you said you were going to have a baby!

Mary:	I did!
	(*Joseph faints again.*)
Mary:	Oh get up!
	(*He wakes up and struggles into a chair.*)
Mary:	Now listen, Joseph, there's nothing to worry about. The Angel Gabriel just popped in and he said I was going to have GOD'S Son.
Joseph:	HE WHAT??!!
Mary:	He said I was going to have God's Son, and you know what that means, don't you?
Joseph:	A party to celebrate?
Mary:	No! You've got to finish putting that shelf up so that you can start work on a cot!
	(*They both exit.*)

Act 2: The journey to Bethlehem

Scene: On the road to Bethlehem. Mary and Joseph enter. Mary is heavily pregnant.

Mary:	How much further is it to Bethlehem?
Joseph:	Not far. I think it's just around the next corner.
Mary:	You've said that at just about every corner for the last hundred miles. When WILL we get there?
Joseph:	Very soon. Look! I can see it now in the distance. (*He points off-stage towards Bethlehem.*) Come on let's get a move on so that we can find somewhere to stay tonight.
	(*They exit. Enter lots of stallholders who create a street scene in Bethlehem.*)
Stallholder 1:	Camels! Luverly camels! Come and buy yer camels 'ere! Good quality second'and camels! All with road tax and a money-back guarantee.
Stallholder 2:	Snakes! Luverly snakes! Come and get yer

	snakes whilst stocks last! Suitable for charming, wearing or eating! Money back if they crush you to death!
Stallholder 3:	Sand! Luverly sand! Fresh from the desert! Turn your back garden into a living representation of the desert with this genuine desert sand! Only 3 shekels a cart load!
	(*The stallholders continue to try and sell their wares, making a lot of noise. Enter Mary and Joseph. The stallholders press round them and try to sell things to them. Except Stallholder 1 who is busy checking his camels and counting his money and fails to notice what's going on.*)
Joseph:	(*Barely audible above the din*) Get off, will yer?! Does any of you have a room to let?! Will you just shut up a minute! Can you let us ...?! ... Do you have ... a room?! ... Look! ... (*Losing his patience and shouting really loudly*) DOES ANYONE HAVE A ROOM WE CAN LET?!
	(*All the stallholders fall silent and stare at him.*)
Stallholder 2:	A room? He wants a room?
	(*All, except Stallholder 1, fall about laughing. Then they gradually exit, still laughing and saying how stupid Joseph is to want a room. Stallholder 1 remains on-stage with Mary and Joseph. He is still counting his money.*)
Joseph:	Do YOU have a place where we could stay?
Stallholder 1:	A place to stay? With everyone in town? You must be joking, pal. (*He starts to leave.*)
Mary:	Please don't leave us. We need somewhere to stay.
Joseph:	That's right. Mary's about to give birth to our baby.
Stallholder 1:	Oh I don't know ... Look I'll tell you what I can do, but it's not much, mind. I've had a good day selling me camels, so

me stall will be empty until I get a fresh delivery in a few days. You can stay in that, if you like. It isn't very nice though, and it stinks of camel.

Mary: That's very kind of you. We can stay there, can't we, Joseph?

Joseph: Yeah. It might not be very clean, but it'll be warmer than being outside. Come on, show us the way. (*They all exit.*)

Act 3: The shepherds

Scene: A Galilean hillside. A group of shepherds enter, followed by their sheep. The shepherds and sheep speak in rhyming couplets; the angels do not.

Shepherd 1: Those sheep, we must look after them –
They have to get to Bethlehem.

Shepherd 2: We've been out here since half past three.
Can't we stop and have some tea?

Shepherd 3: It's time to stop and have a rest.
This spot here will serve us best.

Shepherd 2: Tie the sheep up nice and tight,
Then we can stop here for the night.

Shepherd 1: Tomorrow will be a busy day,
So let's lay down amongst the hay.
(*The shepherds lie down .*)

Sheep 1: Why DO those shepherds talk in verse?

Sheep 2: If they don't stop, it will get WORSE.

Shepherd 3: Be quiet there, you silly sheep!
We all want to get some sleep!

Sheep 2: Those shepherds are a lazy bunch.
But now I think it's time to munch.
(*The sheep start eating. Enter one of the Angels carrying a map and studying it by torchlight.*)

Angel 1: Ah, these must be the shepherds I'm looking for. (*Shines the torch at the shepherds and calls out*) Excuse me! Excuse me! Can I have a word with you guys?
(*The shepherds wake up and are scared by the*

angel. They are all blinded by the light of his torch.)

Shepherd 1: Who brings that blinding little light?
Speak unless you want a fight!

Shepherd 2: Oh do be quiet, you silly fool.
That's an angel – play it cool.

Shepherd 3: (*To the angel*) Please don't hurt me! I've been good –
I've always done just as I should.

Angel 1: Do not be afraid – I've got good news for you. A Saviour has been born in Bethlehem – you'll find him in the secondhand camel stall. He is Christ the Lord.

Shepherd 1: Eh up, folks. This sounds like fun.
We'll be there for breakfast if we run.
(*The shepherds get the sheep and start to leave.*)

Angel 1: Don't go yet. We've got our song to do.
(*Calls off-stage*) Come on, folks! It's time for the song!
(*A whole host of angels enters marching. The next part is a US-army-style chant. The angels march up and down the stage in time to the beat.*)

Angel 1: We are Holy angels bright!
Angels: We are Holy angels bright!
Angel 1: Sent by God to you tonight!
Angels: Sent by God to you tonight!
Angel 1: Down in Bethlehem tonight!
Angels: Down in Bethlehem tonight!
Angel 1: You will see a lovely sight!
Angels: You will see a lovely sight!
Angel 1: Mary's had a baby boy!
Angels: Mary's had a baby boy!
Angel 1: He will bring the world much joy!
Angels: He will bring the world much joy!
Angel 1: Glory to our God on high!
Angels: Glory to our God on high!
Angel 1: Cheerio we must now fly!
Angels: Cheerio we must now fly!

	(*The angels all fly away.*)
Shepherd 3:	That was a lovely little tune – I'm sad it had to end so soon.
Shepherd 1:	Don't just stand there looking sad – We must see this little lad. (*The shepherds and sheep all exit.*)

Act 4: The kings

Scene: About two years later, in the house in Bethlehem where Mary and Joseph are living with Jesus. There are two chairs in the room.

	(*Enter Mary, sweeping up.*)
Mary:	(*Calling off-stage*) Joseph! Joseph! Have you finished putting that shelf up yet? (*Sounds of hammering off-stage.*)
Mary:	Well hurry up! We haven't got all day! (*She carries on sweeping up. Enter Joseph carrying large inflatable hammer.*)
Joseph:	It's OK, Mary. I've finished the shelf. Where's Jesus got to?
Mary:	I've put him to bed. He was worn out, poor lad.
Joseph:	Well, this house is starting to look better. It's certainly better than that old camel stall we stayed in when we first came to Bethlehem.
Mary:	I'll never be able to go near another camel as long as I live. Even after two years, the smell of camels still makes me feel ill.
Joseph:	Have you heard about that star that seems to be coming to Bethlehem?
Mary:	A star coming here? Who? Tom Cruise (*or any current movie star*)?
Joseph:	No, not that kind of star! A star in the sky! There's one that's growing bigger every night, and it looks like it's coming towards Bethlehem.
Mary:	How unusual. But then things have been unusual ever since the Angel Gabriel

	came and told me I was going to have a baby.
Joseph:	They certainly have. Do you remember the shepherds who came to visit?
Mary:	The ones who talked in rhyme? Yes I remember. They said they'd seen some angels who had told them all about Jesus. But what about this star? What IS it?
Joseph:	(*Getting very carried away and acting out this part*) Well, some people say that it's the eye of a giant space creature that's flying towards the earth at a million miles an hour, and when it gets here it'll burn the earth with it's fiery breath, causing the world to explode and we'll all die...!
Mary:	Do you think that's right?
Joseph:	No, I think it's just a star coming towards us. (*Sound of a knock at the door.*)
Mary:	I wonder who that is?
Joseph:	With the way things have been going, I wouldn't be at all surprised if it was some wise men from a far off country who have been studying this mysterious star until it led them right to our door.
Mary:	Stop being so silly and answer the door. (*Joseph exits to answer the door, but almost at once shrieks and comes running back in again.*)
Mary:	Who is it?
Joseph:	It's ... er ... um ... Well, you're not going to believe this but...
Mary:	Who is it?
Joseph:	It's some wise men from a far off country who have been studying this mysterious star until it led them right to our door.
Mary:	Well, don't leave them standing outside – invite them in! (*Joseph exits and then re-enters, walking backwards and bowing a lot. The three wise men follow him in.*)

Joseph: (*Very nervous*) Good afternoon, your highnesses. Do come in. Mary's just about to put the kettle on, so you can stop for a cup of tea if you like. I should leave your camels outside. Make sure you lock them up – it's a bit of a rough area. The chap next door left his camel outside and, the next morning, all it's legs had been stolen and it was left propped up on a pile of bricks. Very nasty it was.

Mary: Stop chattering on like an idiot! Welcome, your highnesses.

Wise Man 1: Greetings! We have come to worship the one who has been born 'King of the Jews'.

Wise Man 2: We have travelled for many months and have brought gifts.

Mary: You must have come to see our son, Jesus. I'm afraid he's asleep at the moment.

Wise Man 3: We really would like to see him, as we want to worship this great King.

Mary: Well, you can come up and see him, only don't make too much noise.

(*They all tiptoe across the stage – the wise men are tiptoeing in an exaggerated fashion but are actually being very noisy. Mary leads the way and Joseph is at the rear.*)

Joseph: (*Tapping Wise Man 3 on the shoulder and whispering loudly*) What gifts have you brought then?

Wise Man 3: (*Whispering loudly*) Gold, frankincense and myrrh.

Mary: (*Whispering loudly*) You're making too much noise! You'll have to take your shoes off.

(*The wise men clap twice and three servants rush in, remove their shoes and rush out again. They resume their tiptoeing. The wise men and Mary tiptoe off-stage.*)

Joseph: (*To himself*) I wonder how they did that clapping thing.

(He tries clapping a few times, nothing happens. He pulls himself up to his full height and claps twice very loudly. The three servants rush in, forcibly remove his shoes and rush out again. Joseph starts to chase after them.)

Joseph: Hey you, come back with my shoes!

Mary: *(Entering)* Shhh! Don't shout, Joseph— you'll wake Jesus.

Joseph: But those servants just stole my shoes!

Mary: Don't worry about that now — I'm too tired.

(They both collapse into the chairs.)

Joseph: Where are the wise men?

Mary: They're still kneeling by Jesus' cot. I told them they could stay the night if they wanted to.

Joseph: Jesus is a special lad, isn't he? I think he's going to change our lives.

Mary: *(Thoughtfully)* I've got a feeling he's going to change the world.

ROCK THE MANGER
a chant

36

Key: A
Theme: Christmas
Based on: Key events in Jesus' life

To Queen's 'We will rock you' with foot-stamping/hand-clapping accompaniment. Chorus sung by several voices, verses sung solo.

It's a baby, it's a boy,
Making no noise
Lying in the hay –
    He's going to be a big man? – No way!
Got an angel's face,
Knows his place,
    Sheep and shepherds all over the place... (singing)

Chorus
We will, we will rock you (x2)

Jesus, you're a man,
Make a big noise,
Preaching in the streets,
    You're gonna change the world some day.
Got love on your face,
Big disgrace,
    Saints and sinners all over the place.

Chorus

Jesus, you're a man,
You're the main man,
    Hanging on the cross – it was the only way.
Got blood on your face,
It's my disgrace.
    I'm not gonna let 'em put you back in your place.

Chorus

Jesus, you're a man,
You're a dead man,
Lying in the grave.
    But you busted out on the third day.
Got a radiant face,
Full of grace,
    Power of Jesus' gonna rock this place.

Chorus (x2)

THE BEGINNING
a poem

37

Key: U
Theme: Easter
Based on: Matthew 26:36 – 27:50

Read dramatically with appropriate emphasis!

In the garden of Gethsemane, under the starlit skies,
The wail of anguished praying caused the followers surprise.
When a self-appointed army burst in upon the scene,
Their lips were curled with malice and their eyes were hard
    and mean,
And one of them stepped forward, greeted Jesus with a kiss
And Jesus asked, 'Now, Judas! Why betray me like this?'
Then the vultures seized him and dragged him down the
    street,
And everybody split the scene and beat a quick retreat.

They took him to the High Priest who questioned him for
    hours.
They wanted proof to nail him – they summoned all their
    powers.
Accusations followed of fraud and blasphemy.
Though many testified, their reports did not agree.
Their mouths spewed out their lies in hisses, barks and spits,
Then they spat and struck at him – those pious hypocrites!
They packed him off to Pilate on a charge of tax evasion,
But Pilate was afraid and resisted their persuasion.

So then they tried King Herod, from Galilee's domain,
Who was hoping for a miracle to keep him entertained.
He asked him many questions, but Jesus held his peace.
So Herod and his soldiers began to mock and tease.
Then on another charge of trying to start a riot,
The chief priests and the elders sent Jesus back to Pilate.
Of the charges laid against him, Jesus offered no defence.
'Crucify him!' yelled the mob, insistent and intense.

Mocked. Stripped.
Flogged. Whipped.
Spat at. Struck.
★Treat like muck.
Crown of thorn.
Jeers and scorn.
Abused. Nailed.
Flesh impaled.
Strength diminished.
'It is finished!'
So he died.
Crucified.
The Beginning.

(*Pronounced like 'threat'.)

BETRAYAL – JUDAS
a rap

Key: L
Themes: Betrayal, Easter
Based on: Matthew 26:14–16, 20–25, 47–50; Mark 14:10–11, 17–21, 43–46; Luke 22:1–6, 21–22, 47–48

Chorus said by several voices. Words in **bold** indicate first beat in the bar.

Judas was a follower in **charge** of all the dough.
When it came to money, he was **always** in the know.
He **liked** to have a flutter on the **Jewish** football pools.
And **when** it came to taxes he **always** bent the rules.
Just before Passover when the **posse** met to nosh,
Judas went to see the priest 'bout **how** to earn some dosh.

Chorus
This **Jesus** gives me hassle, gonna **get** him off my back!
You give me the silver, **I'll** give him the sack.

At the **time** of celebration, as they **sat** to eat their meal,
Jesus knew what was going down, of **Judas'** evil deal.
He **said**, 'One will betray me, the **dude** who shares my
    bread.
It **brings** me grief to say this, but he'll **wish** that he was
    dead.'
Later on that evening as they **sat** out on a hill
Judas kissed his victim – and the **guards** moved in to kill.

Chorus

39 DENIAL – PETER
a rap

Key: L
Themes: Betrayal, Easter, Faith, Fear
Based on: Matthew 26:69–75, Mark 14:66–72, Luke 22:54–62

Chorus said by several voices. Words in bold indicate first beat in the bar.

When the **angry** mob lynched Jesus,
　　Simon **Peter** did a runner.
He was **scared** that if they got him too,
　　Then **he** would be a gonna.
So he **followed** at a distance,
　　Tried to **blend** in with the crowd
And **in** the courtyard by the fire
　　A **girl** said clear and loud,
'Hey, **ain't** you in the posse
　　Of that **Galilean** man?'
But **Peter** said 'No way, José!
　　I **ain't** one of his clan.'

Chorus
'**Don't** you give me hassle,
　　Just get off my back!
I ain't with this Jesus man—
　　Just cut me some slack.'

He **went** out of the gateway
　　To **split** that shady place
When **another** lady asked him,
　　'Hey, **don't** I know your face?'
'Yo **baby**, what yer sayin'?
　　I **don't** know what you're on.'
He **turned** his back and quit the scene—
　　In a **minute** he was gone.

Chorus

Two **dudes** stood by the fire,
　　Told **Peter**, 'Stop yer squawking!
We **know** that you're a Jesus man—
　　We can **tell** by the way you're talking.'
Peter started cursin'—
　　He **said**, 'I've had my fill!
I'm **sick** of people saying stuff!'
　　And **he** went out to chill.

Chorus

He **heard** the cock crow twice—
　　He **thought**, 'Oh no, that bird!'
He **went** away and cried
　　　　'Cos he **remembered** Jesus' word.

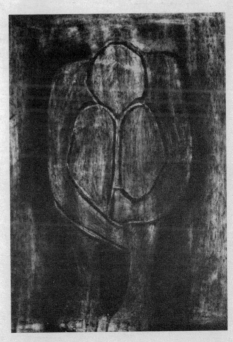

KISSES
a dramatised reading

Key: U
Theme: Betrayal, Easter
Based on: Mark 14:43–49

Reading suggestions

1 As a straightforward poem.
2 With seven readers, each taking a line.
3 Three readers, two saying the lines to each other as if in conversation and one speaking only the final line.
4 Two readers, one reading the narrative and the other the dialogue.

There are 'Aah, goo! Who's a lovely baby then?' type kisses.
There are 'There, there! Don't cry – Mummy'll kiss it better' type kisses.
There are sloppy, yukky, 'Auntie's come to visit' type kisses.
There are 'At last we're alone' type kisses.
There are 'With this ring I thee wed' type kisses.
There is the kiss which says,
'This is the man you want – kill him.'

© Karen Hall 1995